THE GUNSMITH

#33

THE POSSE

Other Books
By
J.R. Roberts

Macklin's Women	Chinatown Hell
The Chinese Gunmen	The Panhandle Search
The Woman Hunt	Wildcat Roundup
The Guns of Abilene	The Ponderosa War
Three Guns for Glory	Trouble Rides a Fast Horse
Leadtown	Dynamite Justice
The Longhorn War	The Posse
Quanah's Revenge	Night of the Gila
Heavyweight Gun	The Bounty Women
New Orleans Fire	Black Pearl Saloon
One-Handed Gun	Gundown in Paradise
The Canadian Payroll	King of the Border
Draw to an Inside Death	The El Paso Salt War
Dead Man's Hand	The Ten Pines Killer
Bandit Gold	Hell with a Pistol
Buckskins and Six-Guns	Wyoming Cattle Kill
Silver War	The Golden Horseman
High Noon at Lancaster	The Scarlet Gun
Bandido Blood	Navaho Devil
The Dodge City Gang	Wild Bill's Ghost
Sasquatch Hunt	The Miner's Showdown
Bullets and Ballots	Archer's Revenge
The Riverboat Gang	Showdown in Raton
Killer Grizzly	When Legends Meet
North of the Border	Desert Hell
Eagle's Gap	The Diamond Gun

For more exciting
E-Books, Audiobooks and MP3 downloads visit us at
www.speakingvolumes.us

THE GUNSMITH

#33

THE POSSE

J.R. ROBERTS

SPEAKING VOLUMES, LLC
NAPLES, FLORIDA
2014

THE GUNSMITH
#33 THE POSSE

Copyright © 1984 by Robert J. Randisi

ISBN 978-1-61232-636-8

To Anna and Christopher

Chapter One

Had he been riding Duke instead of driving the rig the Gunsmith would have noticed the big black gelding's limp much sooner, and the stopover in Phoenix, Texas could have been avoided—along with a peck of trouble. As it was, Clint Adams didn't notice the limp until they were just outside of Phoenix. Duke was obviously favoring his front right hoof, and when Clint lifted it to take a look he found the stone bruise.

"That's great," he said, disgusted with himself as he dropped the hoof to the ground. "Well, we'll just have to stay here longer than we intended, Duke boy, but it ain't your fault, it's mine."

He drove slowly into town so as not to aggravate the bruise any further and went directly to the livery. The liveryman was properly impressed by Duke and promised to take extra good care of him. Satisfied, the Gunsmith took his saddlebags and rifle and went in search of a hotel.

On the main street he found the hotel Phoenix House and registered there. He put his gear in his room and then asked the desk clerk, a young man in his early twenties, where he could get a decent meal. The clerk told Clint he couldn't go wrong eating in the hotel dining room.

True to the clerk's word the lunch Clint ordered was

excellent and the coffee was as black and strong as he liked it. When he paid the waiter he asked directions to the nearest saloon. The waiter told him that the doorway in the rear of the room led to the hotel saloon, which was the finest in town. Since no hotel employee had yet steered him wrong, Clint went through the rear doorway and found himself in an extravagantly furnished establishment with gambling facilities, girls and the longest bar he'd ever seen. He approached the bar, ordered a beer and found that to be excellent too. The only thing that could have topped what he'd had so far would be if he could find a woman who could measure up to what he'd so far experienced.

"Just get into town?" the bartender asked when he brought a second beer on request.

"That's right."

"Staying long?"

"Longer than I'd intended. My horse picked up a stone bruise and I'll have to wait until it heals before I can go on."

"That's too bad," the man said, "but there are worse places you could be stuck."

"I can't argue with you there."

"Got a right nice cathouse at the other end of town, if'n you're lonely," the bartender said. "Or I'm sure one of our girls here would be glad to oblige you."

"Thanks for the offer, but I never pay for my pleasure unless it comes in a glass or on a plate. I can usually do all right without paying for it."

"No offense meant."

"None taken." Clint finished off his beer and declined the barkeep's offer of a third mug on the house. "I'll come back for it," he said. "Right now I think I'll take a look around your town."

Clint left the saloon with the intention of taking a walk around town and then heading back to the hotel for a bath. He didn't expect to walk into the midst of violence and tragic death, but then he was the Gunsmith and was not all that surprised by it either.

Phoenix appeared to be a growing, prosperous town with several banks and saloons and many small stores—hardware, gunshop, general store, dry goods, milliner, haberdasher. He had passed the First Bank of Phoenix and was crossing the street to his hotel when he heard the shots. As he turned, hand streaking for his gun, he saw three, four, five men come running out of the bank. There were five horses tied up there, and Clint had the brief thought that these men were not professional bank robbers; if they had been, one of them would have stayed outside with the horses.

The five men mounted their horses and continued to fire shots into the bank at random. Clint was sure that they were simply slinging lead to keep anyone from rushing out. He continued across the street until he reached the boardwalk in front of the hotel, and there prepared to do his best to stop the men as they rode by.

"Help," someone finally shouted from inside the bank, "we've been robbed!"

As the men rode toward him Clint eased his gun out of his holster and prepared to sling some lead of his own, but as he did he saw from the corner of his eye a little girl running into the street.

"No!" he shouted, but his anguished cry came too late. His gun forgotten, he watched in helpless horror as the five men rode over the little girl, trampling her into the ground. He had been too far away to make any move toward saving her, but had been close enough to hear the sounds of the horses' hooves crushing the life from her.

By the time he recovered from the shock the five men were riding past him. He fired two shots after them and was sure that he had hit someone, but all five remained on their horses and disappeared in clouds of dust.

Holstering his gun he ran into the street to the little girl even though he knew damned well that she was dead. She looked like tattered rag doll, except that rag dolls don't bleed.

Suddenly, a woman was standing beside him screaming, staring down at the child with her fists pressed against her face. Her eyes were wide and her skin milky white with shock, and there could be no doubt but that she was the little girl's mother.

"Ma'am," he said, helplessly. He did not know whether

to back away from her or put his arms around her. He could see even under those circumstances that she was young and pretty, probably exactly what the little girl would have grown up to look like.

He did not have to make a move toward her, for abruptly the street was filled with people, one of whom was an older woman who took the young mother in her arms and led her away, crooning to her.

A man wearing a sheriff's tin stood over the little girl, then called out for someone to get a blanket. When he had one he wrapped her in it and picked her up, but before taking her away he turned to Clint and said, "Mister, I'm gonna want to talk to you. You were the closest one to those jaspers, and the only man who got off a shot. Mind stopping by my office a little later?"

"Not at all, Sheriff. I'll be there."

The sheriff nodded, then walked away with the dead little girl seemingly weightless in his arms. It was as if she had not only lost her life, but all substance as well.

The Gunsmith holstered his gun and changed his previous plans. To hell with a bath—what he needed now was a drink.

Chapter Two

He had one whiskey and two beers, and then left the saloon to go to the sheriff's office and get that over with. Thinking about the little girl, he reflected that that particular moment had been one of the few times in his life when he had been so stunned that he could not react. If that had not been the case, he probably would have been able to bring down one or two of the fleeing men. As it stood now, the sheriff had virtually nothing to work with, unless someone in the bank had recognized one of the men. Otherwise all the lawman had was a dusty trail, and if he didn't get a posse together fast, it would be a cold trail as well.

When he reached the sheriff's office he saw by the sign outside that the man's name was John Russell. Clint entered the office without knocking, and Sheriff Russell looked up from his desk, where he was studying flyers. The sheriff was tall and slim, with dark hair and a bushy mustache, probably in his early to mid-forties.

"Got a partial description of one man from a teller, but she was so shook up who knows what she remembered and what she imagined." He gathered the flyers together in one pile and set them aside. "I recognized you out there, Adams."

"I thought you might have."

"I'm surprised you didn't bring at least one of them down."

"You mean you're disappointed."

"Yeah, that too." Russell ran a slim-fingered hand over his face, and it made a raspy sound against his beard stubble. "It's horrible! I knew that little girl, you know. And her mother. Pretty little things, both of them." Russell waved one hand and went on. "I'm . . . shook up, and I don't mind admitting it."

"I know how you feel."

"You were the closest to the—the action," Russell said, trying to find a word that wouldn't conjure up the horrible memory all over again. "Did you see anything that might help me?"

Shaking his head Clint said, "I'm sorry, Sheriff. I saw five men riding toward me, and then I saw that little girl. After that . . ." He trailed off and shrugged helplessly.

"Yeah."

"How's the mother?"

"In shock, that's how. The doctor gave her something to make her sleep, but she's got to wake up sometime. That little girl was all she had. Her man was killed a few months back, and now this. I don't know if Janet can handle this."

"She'll handle it," Clint said, "with help."

"She'll have plenty of that," Russell said, and Clint wondered whether the man meant himself or just other friends.

"Have you got anything else you think will help me?" the sheriff asked hopefully.

"I'm sorry, Sheriff. I wish I had. I wish to God I had."

"Yeah, well . . . I guess you can go, then." As Clint turned to leave Russell asked, "Are you gonna be in town long?"

"Couple of days, I guess. Depends on how quick my horse heals." He told Russell what had happened, and Russell nodded in sympathy.

"Is that the big black I've heard so much about?"

Over the past few years, Duke had become almost as famous as the Gunsmith himself.

"That's the one."

Russell nodded and picked up the flyers again. "Thanks for coming in, Adams."

"Not at all, Sheriff. Good luck."

"I'm not the one who's gonna need good luck," Russell said. "Those five will, when I catch up to them. That much I swear!"

Clint didn't envy those five men when—and if—Russell did catch up with them. The sheriff may not have admitted it, but there was something very personal about the way he was reacting. Clint felt outrage, but the sheriff seemed to feel just plain rage. The Gunsmith hoped that Sheriff Russell would know how to handle that, because that much rage could get a man killed.

Chapter Three

Clint saw the sheriff again much sooner than he expected to. He came out of his bath and found the lawman waiting for him in his room.

"How did you get in here?"

"This badge rates certain privileges. You ought to remember that, you wore one long enough."

"That was a long time ago," Clint said, putting on a clean shirt.

"I was hoping maybe you'd be about ready to put one on again."

Clint hadn't worn a badge for quite some time now, and if he could help it, it was going to stay that way. "I don't find myself with the urge very often. What did you have in mind?"

"I need somebody who'll be some good in a posse."

"Got a shortage of volunteers?"

"Not hardly. Got too dang many, and most of them are storekeepers and such. I could use a man who knows his way around."

"Sorry, Sheriff, but as soon as my horse is fit I'm riding out, and for that matter there is the fact that my horse is lame."

"That wouldn't be such a problem if you'd agree," the sheriff declared in something of a huff. Standing up he said,

"Guess you just ain't the man I thought you was."

"I guess not, Sheriff. Sorry."

When he saw that he couldn't even shame the Gunsmith into joining the posse, Sheriff Russell gave up and left.

Clint walked over to the window and looked down at the street. He could see the spot where the little girl had lain after she'd been trampled. After a moment he saw Sheriff Russell cross the street and head for his office. He waited long enough for the door to the sheriff's office to open again and then, as he'd suspected, out walked the little girl's mother. With a purposeful stride she crossed the street and headed for the hotel, and the Gunsmith knew he was about to have company again.

He left his room and hurried down the steps so that he would meet the young woman in the lobby.

"Mr. Adams," she called when she saw him.

"I'm not running away, ma'am," he told her. "Maybe we should go into the dining room and have some coffee while we talk."

"You were expecting me? Did Sheriff Russell—"

"He didn't have to. Shall we?"

She preceded him into the dining room where they took a table and ordered some coffee.

"My name is Janet Wilson. My little girl's name was . . . was Jenny."

"Mrs. Wilson, it isn't hard for me to guess why you're here. The sheriff must have told you some things about me, but I'm sure he's a capable man. He'll find the men who . . . who—"

"I know John—the sheriff—is a capable man, Mr. Adams, but you are the Gunsmith. There are very few men like you in the world. Why, you've killed more men—I—I need someone like you to—to—"

"Mrs. Wilson," Clint interrupted her, "my gun is not for hire. I am not a killer for hire, no matter what you might have heard about me."

"I'm—I'm sorry," she stammered. "I didn't mean to—to insult you in any way. I'm just—"

"There's no need for you to explain anything to me, ma'am. I know how it is to lose someone you love."*

"But a child? A little girl who hadn't even begun to live her life yet? Mr. Adams, I'm just a schoolteacher. I can't begin to understand what motivates a man like you, but you *saw* what they did to my little girl. You don't mean to tell me that you can forget that?"

"Ma'am, I will never forget what I saw out on that street today—"

"Then how can you just ride away without doing anything? I'm sorry, Mr. Adams, but I just can't understand you. I—I can't sit here—"

She stood up hastily and the tears were finally coming. He was amazed that she had been able to hold them back that long. She bolted from the table and ran from the room, leaving the other diners staring at Clint, wondering what kind of a brute he must be to have upset her so.

When the waitress came with the coffee and two cups he told her, "Just one cup. The lady had to leave."

When she left he poured himself a cup and started to think. She obviously had preconceptions about the kind of man he was, and whether or not that was due to something the sheriff had said he didn't know. He only knew that the accusing look in her eyes had bothered him.

"Goddamn woman," he muttered. He grabbed his hat, jammed it onto his head and went to tell the sheriff that he would join his posse.

"That's great," Sheriff Russell said. "I figured you'd come around."

"Yeah," the Gunsmith said sourly, "you figured that when you set Janet Wilson loose on me."

"I didn't think you'd be able to say no to her."

"Well, I changed my mind, Sheriff, but not for any reason that I'd be able to explain to you."

"That's all right with me, Mr. Adams," the lawman said, "as long as you changed it."

*The Gunsmith #25: North of the Border

"Well, it's going to be dark soon," Clint said. "When do you want to start?"

"In the morning," Russell said. "No point going out after them in the dark. We should be able to pick up their trail come morning. You can use the time to pick yourself out a good horse. Tell Charlie at the stable that he's to supply you with one as part of a lawful posse."

Clint nodded and started to leave.

"Wait," Russell said, opening his desk drawer. "I'll deputize you and give you a badge."

"No."

"What?"

"You can deputize me along with the rest of the posse in the morning, but you don't expect them all to wear badges, so I won't either."

"I don't have enough badges to give them all one, but—"

"I'll ride with your posse, Sheriff, but I won't wear a badge. Take it or leave it."

"I'll take it," Russell said, but he was looking at the Gunsmith with a strange expression on his face.

"That's fine. There's one more thing."

"What's that?"

"You're pretty emotional about this, whether you admit it or not. When we catch those men, I won't be party to lynching them. They're to be brought back here for trial."

Russell's face turned red and if looks could kill the Gunsmith would have been a dead man. "I been a lawman a long time, Adams. I do things according to the law."

"Just speaking my mind, Sheriff, that's all."

"Well, then, I'll speak mine. You were a lawman once, but now you been riding without a badge for a long time. You've got a mighty big reputation, earned or not, and I won't be a party to any killing to add to your reputation. Do we understand each other?"

"I guess we do, Sheriff. I'll see you in the morning."

"You know what to bring with you."

Without replying Clint turned and left the man's office. He headed for the livery to pick out a horse, hoping that the liveryman was going to be able to fix him up with something decent. He didn't relish going after five desperate men on a piece of fly bait.

That's what happened when you were used to riding a horse like Duke. He kind of ruined you for any other animal.

Chapter Four

As he had expected, Duke was not anywhere near being ready to ride so he simply picked out the best horse he could find—a rangy gray gelding about Duke's age—and then went in search of some sort of distraction.

In the hotel saloon he found a poker game with some pretty bad players, and after a while he was winning so regularly that it began to get boring.

That was when the woman walked in.

She stood at the entrance and began to survey the room, giving him an opportunity to look her over. She was tall, small breasted but full in the hips and thighs. Her face was thin but pretty, and her hair was long and brown. She looked to be about twenty-eight or so. She was wearing a workshirt and jeans, and the forty-five on her hip made her even more interesting. The people in the saloon seemed to know her, because no one else but him was looking at her.

She continued to look around the room until her eyes fell on him, at which point she seemed to nod to herself and walked to the bar. She ordered a beer and when the bartender brought it she turned with the mug in hand, leaned her elbows on the bar and watched the game—or *him*.

After he lost a couple of hands he decided that she was occupying his mind too much for him to play anymore. He collected his winnings and excused himself from the game.

Even though the bar was long and there was plenty of

room, he decided to go up and stand right next to her. Since she was being bold—he had decided that she had been watching *him* and not just the game—he decided to be just as bold.

He ordered a beer then looked at her; she was standing in the same position but was looking directly at him.

"You seemed to be doing all right for yourself," she said.

"You mean in the game?"

"What else would I mean?"

"I do pretty good," he said, accepting his beer from the bartender. "If I didn't, I wouldn't bother."

"You don't bother with things you're not good at?"

"There's not much point to that, is there?"

Instead of answering she said, "Why did you stop, then?"

"I stopped because I couldn't concentrate," he said, deciding to be honest about it.

"Why not?"

"Something was distracting me."

"What?"

"You."

She grinned a little and said, "You find me distracting?"

"To say the least."

"Why?"

"I'm being honest and you're fishing for compliments."

She paused a moment and then said, "You're right. Since you're being so honest, I suppose I should be."

She turned toward the bar, put her mug on it and leaned against him so that their shoulders were touching.

"I noticed you as soon as I walked in the door."

That was a lie, because she had surveyed a good portion of the room before her eyes found him, but he said, "Is that a fact?"

"Yes, it is."

"Well, I noticed you as soon as you walked in too. What do you think we should do about it?"

"Well, we could go somewhere and get better acquainted."

"Lady, I've got to tell you that when a woman says something like that to me, there's only one thing it could mean."

"Well, I guess I mean it then, don't I?"

"Your room or mine?"

"Well, since I don't live in town I guess that means we'll have to use yours."

"Fine," he said, still not sure whether or not she was serious. "Let's go."

They left the saloon through the door that connected it to the hotel and went to his room without exchanging another word. When they reached his door he stopped. "You're sure about this?"

"Mister, I'm not a schoolgirl," she said without any hint of anger. It was just a statement of fact, and one that he agreed with entirely.

He opened the door and allowed her to enter ahead of him, then closed it behind him.

"Would you like the lamp?" he asked.

"Why not? We might as well both see what we're getting."

He turned it up just enough so that they could see. "Names?"

"Mine's Demi."

"I'm Clint."

"I'd say we better start getting our clothes off, Clint, or we aren't going to get anywhere."

Without waiting to see how he reacted she started to unbutton her shirt. When that was done she took off her gun and loosened the belt of her pants so that she could pull her shirttail out and remove the shirt. This bared her breasts so that he could see that they were small but full and rounded, with large dark brown nipples.

Up to this point Clint's mind had been occupied with why this woman had come into the saloon looking for him and what she was up to, but the more clothes she removed, the less he thought about that. By the time she was fully naked, he was fully aroused.

"What about you?" she asked, putting her hands on her hips.

He removed his gunbelt and hung it on the bedpost, then removed the remainder of his clothing. Next, he walked up to her and touched his palms to her nipples. She closed her eyes at the contact and let her breath out slowly so that he could smell the beer she had drunk. She placed her hands on his hips, then slid them around so that she gripped his buttocks. As she pulled him to her, her mouth opened and he captured it with his. Her tongue was hot and eager, searching his mouth until it found his. His massive erection was prodding her in the belly now, and she slid her hands from his buttocks and took hold of him. With her thumbs she felt the head of his cock, and he slid his hands down so that he could cup her firm buttocks.

"The bed," she said against his mouth and they moved and fell on it together without bothering to turn it down.

They were both eager now, and there was nothing tentative about the way they explored each other's bodies. She was obviously very skilled in the art of lovemaking and had her preferences about the way to do things. She seemed to enjoy being on top, and when they finally decided to get around to doing the deed, it was with her in that position. She raised her hips and was slick enough for him to slide right in.

Then she began to ride him with her hands flat on his chest. He reached up for her and pulled her down so that he could reach her breasts with his mouth. He sucked on her breasts while she continued to move up and down on him. When she exploded into her climax he let himself go too, spewing his seed into her with incredible force.

"Oh, I can feel *that*," she said happily, milking him for more and more.

He held her buttocks until he was finished filling her and then slid his hands up the elegant curve of her back. She kissed him softly and slid off of him so that she was lying next to him.

"Not disappointed, I hope," she said.

"I don't think either one of us is."

"No, I guess not." Then she rose abruptly from the bed and started getting dressed.

"Is that it?" he asked. "We're through?"

She looked down at him speculatively and said, "No, I

guess you're not through, not by a long shot . . . but maybe another time. I have somewhere else to go.''

"Husband? Boyfriend?''

She shook her head and said, "Neither. I want to go and be with my sister.''

"Oh?'' he asked, and it suddenly dawned on him why she looked so familiar. "Is your last name Wilson?''

"No, it's Templeton,'' she said, "but you're on the right track. My sister's last name is Wilson.''

"Janet Wilson?''

"Yes.''

He sat up in bed now and said, "You came into that saloon looking for me tonight. Why?''

"I didn't think I fooled you,'' she said, putting on her gun belt. "The sheriff told my sister that you were riding with the posse tomorrow. I am too.''

"You volunteered?''

"That's right,'' she said, defensively. "My sister and I are very different, Mr. Adams. *She's* the schoolteacher, not me.''

"Do you know how to use that gun?''

"If I didn't, it wouldn't make any sense for me to wear it, would it?''

"That still doesn't explain why you came looking for me.''

She walked to the door and said, "My sister came to talk to you yesterday and formed an opinion about you.'' She turned the knob on the door and said, "I have my own ways of forming opinions, Clint. See you in the morning.''

Chapter Five

When Clint got to the stable the next morning there were a number of other members of the posse there as well. He mounted up and rode over to the sheriff's office where about twenty more armed men, on and off horses, were waiting. From the way they were handling their guns, it wasn't hard for Clint to pick out the shopkeepers from the ones who really knew what a gun was for.

The sheriff came out of his office as Clint rode up and waved for him to come into the office. Clint tied off his horse and dismounted, looking for Demi Templeton. Apparently she hadn't arrived yet.

When he entered the office the sheriff said, "I'm glad you're here, Clint. I wanted to talk to you before we rode out."

There were three other men in the office with him, all of whom were wearing deputies' badges. Russell very quickly introduced Clint to them. One of them was his regular deputy, Cal Ramsey, and the other two were obviously men he felt were capable enough to wear a badge, Sam Dodger and Willie Akens.

"We five are probably the ones most used to using our guns, so I thought we should talk before we moved out. There are about twenty men out there and I'm going to go out and choose eleven of them who I don't think will get in our way too much. I'm not taking the others because they're just as likely to shoot off a toe—or shoot one of us—as not.''

"Why don't just the five of us go?'' Cal Ramsey asked.

"I want the others along for appearances as much as anything else,'' Russell explained. "When we catch up to these men, a show of force might come in handy.''

Ramsey didn't seem to agree, but didn't discuss it further.

"If we have to split up at any point, I'll choose one of you to head up the other half of the posse. I'll expect my choice to go unchallenged. I won't be in any position or mood to deal with personalities out there.''

There was no dissent, although Clint did notice a look on Ramsey's face that said if and when that time arose, he expected to be the one put in charge. Deputy Ramsey was fairly young, in his mid-twenties, and Clint wondered how much experience he had with the job. In any case, either one of the other two men was old enough to have had more experience.

The sheriff continued. "Now even with the people I pick we might end up with a few trigger-happy souls. We're going to have to make sure that no shooting gets done that I don't order. I'm counting on you more experienced men to set an example.''

There was no argument with that either.

"All right, then. Let's get out there.''

"Can I talk to you a second before we go outside?'' Clint asked as the others started for the door.

"What about?''

"Somebody named Demi Templeton.''

The sheriff frowned and asked, "How do you know Demi?''

"I met her last night. She said she's Janet Wilson's sister.''

"That's right.'' Russell seemed to tense up as soon as Clint mentioned Demi's name.

"She also said she's riding with the posse. I take it she'll be one of those you don't pick.''

"Not at all. In fact, Demi will be one of the first. She's better with a gun than most men I've seen.''

"I've known capable women before, Sheriff, so don't get the idea I'm objecting on that count."

"But you are objecting?"

"She's the dead girl's aunt."

"Demi's not the emotional type."

"That may be, but—"

"This is my posse, Adams," Russell said, reminding Clint who was in charge. "I'm not in love with the idea of having Demi along either, but I need as many capable guns as I can get and her gun is at least that."

"All right," Clint said, backing off. "It's your posse."

"Exactly, and I'd like to get it under way."

Outside, Clint stayed in the background while Russell addressed the waiting men, explaining that he was taking some and leaving some, and couldn't afford the time to argue after his choices were made. Clint noticed that Demi Templeton had shown up, and he also noticed that Russell waited until the end before he chose her.

A few people tried to argue, but Russell put them down hard and turned away from them. He told his posse roughly what he had told Clint and the others in his office: He was in charge, and would not take kindly to any arguments or any premature shooting. Russell finally gave the order to mount up, and the posse got under way.

Early on Demi rode in the back, but eventually she drew up alongside Clint.

"Good morning," she said. "You're not angry with me, are you?"

"Why should I be angry with you?"

"Well, that wasn't a very nice thing I did to you last night."

"You think not?" he asked, looking at her. "I thought it was real nice, myself."

He had the satisfaction of seeing her face color as she said, "I didn't mean that."

"What *did* you mean, then?"

"I meant the reason I did it."

"To evaluate me? I did some evaluating of my own, so I guess we're even enough."

"I guess you *are* angry."

"No, I'm not."

"Well, if that's true, then I'm glad. It will making working together much easier."

"The sheriff tells me that you can handle that gun pretty well."

"I told you that last night."

"I just hope you know *when* to use it as well as how."

She straightened her back and said, "Don't you worry, Mr. Gunsmith. You're not the only person in the world who knows how to use a gun. I'll do my part."

With that she spurred her horse on and caught up to Sheriff Russell, riding alongside him for a while. Clint wondered about Russell's relationship with the two sisters. If there was something between Russell and Demi Templeton, he hoped it would not get in the way while they were riding together on this posse.

Clint had known capable women before, as he had told Russell—one in particular, the bounty hunter Lacy Blake*—but it remained to be seen how Demi Templeton compared with someone of Lacy's abilities.

At that moment, some fifty miles closer to the New Mexico border, five riders pulled to a stop for a brief rest.

"Lon is bleedin' bad," Johnny Hogan said to his older brother Clyde.

"We can't stop for him," Clyde said.

"We been riding all night, Clyde—" Johnny started, but his brother cut him off.

"And we should have made better time," Clyde said. "Lon is slowing us down as it is, Johnny. You know there's got to be a posse on our trail, and you want to stop and rest?"

Johnny wanted to argue with his brother, but he had never been able to do that for very long, even when they were kids.

Johnny Hogan was twenty-one, tall and slender with blond hair and gray eyes, while his brother Clyde, twenty-six, was a big and hulking blond, with a flat head that had earned him

*The Gunsmith #24: Killer Grizzly

the nickname Hammerhead when he was a child. The name had stuck, but no one called him that to his face anymore, not since he had killed four men for doing just that.

The other three men in the gang were Dan Clayton, Matt Daniels and the wounded man, Lon Shaw.

"What's the holdup?" Matt Daniels asked, riding up alongside the two brothers.

"My brother's complaining about Lon not having time to rest."

"Then let him stay behind with him. I'm not risking my neck for him or anybody else. I ain't stopping until my horse drops, and then I'm just gonna steal another one and get going again. That posse's gonna be riding us hard, especially after your brother rode down that little girl—"

"I didn't see her, I told you!" Johnny Hogan shouted, growing red in the face. "I didn't do it on purpose."

"Nobody said you did," Clyde Hogan said. "Go back and check on Lon, Johnny. Go on." As Johnny rode off Clyde turned to Matt Daniels and said, "Don't keep mentioning that, Matt! The kid feels bad enough as it is."

"I don't care how bad he feels, Clyde. He drove that little girl into the ground and that's why this posse's gonna be extra hard to shake. You know that."

"I know it, but I also know it can't be helped. What's done is done."

"Look, if you're thinking about stopping to rest, then give me my cut now so I can keep going."

"I ain't saying that," Clyde Hogan said, "and we ain't splitting the money up until we get where we're headed."

Clyde pulled his horse around and rode back to where his brother was talking to Lon Shaw.

"How's it going, Lon?"

Shaw's face was white, his skin like wax, and Clyde knew he was in shock. He'd seen it before. "I'm all right, Clyde, honest. Don't stop on my account. Don't leave me behind."

"Nobody's leaving you behind, Lon, but one of us could stay with you awhile if you want to rest."

"No! I want to keep going. I'll be all right."

"That's it, then," Clyde said to his brother. "We move."

Clyde rode up to the front and the five men started riding again. Hammerhead Hogan knew that if Lon Shaw got off his horse, he wasn't ever going to get on it again unless he was slung across his saddle.

And he knew that Shaw knew that too.

Chapter Six

They were only out a day when the problem Sheriff Russell had anticipated arose. He waited until they had made camp and gotten something to eat before bringing it up.

He was seated with Clint, Cal Ramsey, Sam Dodger, Willie Akens and Demi Templeton when he said, "There are two ways they could have gone from this point."

"Mexico or New Mexico," Demi said.

Russell looked at her and nodded. "We'll have to split up here, and since I'm sheriff I'll take my men and go to Mexico."

"You don't have any authority there," Clint said.

"And you'd have even less," Russell said.

"We're going in after them anyway?" Ramsey asked.

"Yes. Clint, I want you to lead the second posse."

Cal Ramsey's head came sharply around at that, but he didn't argue.

"Why me?" Clint asked, because he'd noticed Ramsey's reaction.

"You've got the most experience. If anybody objects, it's too damn bad." Russell got up to go to the fire and get more coffee, and Ramsey followed. Akens and Dodger both excused themselves and said that they were going to turn in.

"He made the right decision," Demi said to Clint.

"I know, but I didn't want to be a part of this posse in the first place, and now I'm heading up half of it. Some of these people aren't going to take kindly to that job being given to a stranger.''

''Especially Cal Ramsey?''

''You noticed that, huh?''

''I noticed. Cal's arguing with the sheriff right now.''

They looked over toward the fire and saw Russell and Ramsey in a heated conversation.

''He's not going to get anywhere arguing with John,'' she said.

''How well do you and your sister know the sheriff?'' Clint asked.

''Any particular reason you want to know that?''

''He tenses up whenever I mention either one of you.''

''John wanted to marry Janet some years back, but then she went and married Bill Wilson. I don't think he ever fully accepted their marriage. He was always around, and Bill didn't like it much.''

''What happened to Wilson?''

She looked right at him and said, ''Somebody killed him . . . and I know what you're thinking.''

''I'm not thinking anything,'' he lied.

''You're thinking that maybe John Russell killed Wilson.''

That's what he was thinking. ''Was he sheriff then?''

''He was, but that's not the reason I don't think he killed him.''

''What is, then? Any interest in him yourself?''

''I won't pretend that I wasn't interested in him once, but not anymore. No, I just don't—I don't think he killed him, that's all.''

''That's a good reason.''

''He knows that Janet would never forgive him if she ever found out that he did. He still hopes that she'll marry him, and now she might.''

''Why do you say that?''

''Jenny's death has devastated her. She's going to need someone to lean on to keep from going to pieces, and John is going to be around.''

''He may also be the man to bring Jenny's killers to

justice," Clint added. "That ought to count for something. I suppose that's why he's determined to catch them, even if it means going into Mexico."

"I guess. And he really loved Jenny—I think he saw her as the child he and Janet would have had."

Russell had ended his conversation with Ramsey and left him standing at the fire, still obviously dissatisfied with the current turn of events.

As Russell started toward them Clint said, "I guess I'll be turning in."

"Don't go—" she said, but Russell had come within earshot before she could continue, so she stopped short. It was obvious that she didn't want to be alone with him, though, so Clint stayed where he was.

"Trouble?" he asked when the sheriff sat next to them.

"No," he said firmly. "You better turn in, Adams. We're going to get an early start in the morning."

Clint looked at Demi, who shook her head slightly and said, "In a while."

Russell frowned at Clint, then at Demi, before standing up and saying, "Well, I ain't gonna stay up all night jawing," and went off to set up his bedroll.

"Thanks," Demi said.

"Why don't you want to be alone with him?"

"Because he doesn't want to marry me, he just . . . wants me."

"What's wrong with that?"

"I don't want him. He makes me . . . uncomfortable."

Clint had the feeling—and it was a strong one—that Demi Templeton really did think that John Russell had killed her brother-in-law.

"You want me to set up my bedroll here?" he asked. When she looked at him he said, "My intentions are purely honorable."

"Too bad," she said, smiling. "I would appreciate it, yes."

When they both had their bedrolls set up, only a couple of feet apart, Clint became aware of Russell watching them.

"It seems strange to me that the man who wants to marry your sister would still be after you."

"I'm sure he's only interested in being with me once. It's like a curiosity, you know? It gnaws at you."

"Glad I don't have that problem," he said. "I'd hate to have it gnawing at me this whole trip."

"You wouldn't have to," she said, and turned over so that her back was to him.

Clint put his hands behind his head, wondering how Russell was going to split the posse up in the morning. Would he send Ramsey with Clint? Keep Demi with him? Clint would prefer it the other way around. He and Demi had become friends, but he had the feeling that he and Cal Ramsey would never make it to that point.

Chapter Seven

In the morning Russell told everyone which group they would be in. As Clint had feared, Russell assigned Ramsey to ride with him, while the lawman kept Demi in his group.

Several people—Demi among them—went over to talk to the sheriff after he finished his announcement. None of them had any luck with the lawman except Demi. After their rather lengthy conversation, Russell told Dodger that he would ride with the first group, while Demi would be in Clint's.

"How did you manage that?" Clint asked her as they were mounting up to get moving.

"I told him the truth," she said, "that I thought his mind would be on me if I went with him, and not on his work."

"You told him that? How did he react?"

"Not well, but as you can see I got my way."

"I'll bet you're used to that, aren't you?"

She gave him a sly grin and said, "You ought to know."

As they were getting ready to move out Cal Ramsey rode over to Clint.

"Adams, I want you to know I ain't happy about the sheriff picking you to lead this part of the posse."

"That makes two of us, Cal, but I hope that doesn't mean that we won't be able to work with each other. To tell you the truth, I'm going to have to lean pretty heavily on you, and I'd like to know that I can count on you."

Taken aback by such a confession from The Gunsmith,

Ramsey relented a bit and said, "I'll do my job."

"Good. I was hoping you'd say that."

As they started off Clint was satisfied that Ramsey was somewhat mollified by his remarks, but he didn't know how long that would last.

Demi rode up next to him and said, "You sure you never thought about becoming a politician?"

"Too much horse manure in that job."

"Well, you didn't sound like you were any short on it a minute ago."

Clint looked back at Ramsey, who was talking with a couple of riders, and said, "I only hope he keeps his resentment from interfering with his work."

"I'll keep an eye on him."

"Is he another one of your would-be beaus?"

She made a face at him and said, "Hardly."

"Tell me something."

"What?"

"What makes you and your sister so different?"

"I don't know. We both got the same education, which, I guess, means I could have become a teacher too if I wanted—which I didn't! Janet's younger, and she was always the gentler of the two of us. I was the one who protected her as we were growing up. I guess that had something to do with it."

"What did you think of her choice of a husband?"

"Bill? He was all right. He worked hard, and he loved her and Jenny. Bill was all right."

"How did he die? What were the circumstances?"

"He was shot one night after he closed the store—he ran the general store—on his way home. He was shot in the back."

"That doesn't sound like the sheriff's style."

She looked at him sharply and said, "I told you I didn't think John did it!"

"Yeah, I know what you *told* me."

She worried her lip some, and then said, "All right, so I think about it now and then. It's only natural."

"Hey, you don't have to explain it to me. Just don't feel so guilty about it. It's only natural."

"I guess."

To get her mind off it Clint said, "Fill me in on some of the people we've got riding with us, will you?"

He listened while she ran it down for him, telling him that there were about three men who were regulars whenever a posse was needed.

"This is the first time something as bad as this has happened," she said. "It seems to have brought something out in these people. Take Olle Bjorkman, for instance. Most of the time he's just a sweet old Swedish bear, but this has gotten even him angry. He's not too good with a gun, but I've seen him whip five men, so he won't be in the way."

Clint believed that—Bjorkman was six and a half feet if he was an inch, and beneath him his horse looked like a burro.

Originally there had been sixteen in the posse, and now that they'd split, Clint and the sheriff were leading posses of eight each. Russell's show of force had withered some, but Clint still felt that he had wounded at least one man, and maybe that man was dead by now, which meant they'd be tracking four.

"Who's the tracker in this group?" he asked Demi, since up to that point the sheriff himself had been reading sign.

She grinned widely. "Why do you think I'm up here with you?"

He laughed. "Demi, you're a bundle of surprises."

"Wait until you see me shoot. I know you think that because I'm a woman—"

"Whoa, that just isn't so. I've know women before who were good with a gun."

"Oh? Who?"

He told her about Lacy Blake, the woman with whom he had once hunted a giant grizzly,* and she listened intently as he described Lacy's abilities.

"What does she look like?"

"She's very attractive."

"Oh? Are you . . . good friends with her?" When he

*The Gunsmith #24:Killer Grizzly

looked at her she added, "Well, you asked me about John Russell."

"Lacy and I are friends."

"Like you and I are friends?"

"Are we friends?"

"I'd like to think so."

"All right, we're friends."

"You're avoiding my question."

"Which one?" When she opened her mouth to argue he said, "All right, Lacy and I got to be . . . good friends."

"I don't think I like that."

"Well, don't let it keep you awake nights."

"I've never known a man who could keep me awake nights," she said stiffly.

"You didn't give me half a chance last night," he complained, and if she had been angry, it faded and she laughed.

"Let me ask you one."

"You mean another one," she said, correcting him.

"All right, another one. Where did you get the name Demi?"

She made a face and said, "You really want to know that?"

"I'm curious. You wouldn't want it to gnaw at me, would you?"

"Well, if you put it that way . . ." She took a deep breath and said, "My parents named me Demetria."

"Why would they want to go and do a thing like that?"

"They had both read a lot about the ancient Romans, and if they had a boy they were going to call him Demetrius. They had me, so I ended up with . . . that name."

"And you shortened it to Demi."

"As a child I couldn't say my name and it always came out Demi, so that's what they started to call me. Thank God."

"Demetria Templeton," Clint said, trying it on for size. "You know, I think I like that."

"If you call me that . . ." She left the threat unfinished.

"I can't think of anything bad enough to threaten you with."

"Don't worry, I won't call you—that name."

"Promise?"

"I promise."

For the remainder of that morning she impressed him with her ability to read sign.

"It looks like we're the lucky ones," she said at one point.

"They could have split up," he said, "three one way and two another."

"That's possible, I guess."

"The sheriff will have to play it that way, just to be on the safe side."

"Yeah, but this looks like more than three horses to me."

"All right, let's keep going. Russell might give up at some point and try to catch up to us."

As they got close to the New Mexico border Demi spotted something that made her call them to a halt.

"What is it?"

"I'm not sure," she said. She dismounted and squatted down on the ground, running her hand over the sand. "If I'm not mistaken it looks like blood." She stood up and walked back to stand beside Clint's horse. "It looks like they may have stopped here for a few moments, long enough for someone to lose enough blood for me to notice."

"I knew I hit one," he said.

"He must be hit pretty bad too. Of course, this could be from some animal."

"Maybe, but let's hope it's not. Sooner or later a wounded man is going to slow them down."

"Or be left behind."

"Clyde!"

Clyde Hogan stopped his horse and looked back to see what had caused his brother to call him. Lon Shaw had dropped dangerously far behind them, which concerned Johnny more than it did anyone else. Johnny had brought Shaw into the gang; Shaw was his friend. Yet Johnny was Clyde's brother; Clyde couldn't leave Johnny behind with Shaw, knowing that he might be caught.

Clyde rode back to Johnny and said, "Look, kid—"

"He's gonna die, isn't he, Clyde?"

"It looks that way, Johnny."

Johnny looked at Clyde and said, "We can't let him die alone, Clyde."

"Johnny, nobody's gonna stay behind with him."

"I will, Clyde."

"I can't let you do that."

"But, Clyde—"

"Forget it, Johnny! There's a posse coming fast—"

"But, Clyde—"

Clyde's right hand shot out and connected with the side of his brother's face. "Aw, Johnny, can't you see I don't want you gettin' caught?"

"Sure, Clyde, I see that," Johnny said, looking down at the ground.

Clyde looked at the others and said, "Is Lon carrying any of the money?"

"No, Clyde," Matt Daniels said, "just you and me."

"All right," Clyde said, looking at his brother, "let's keep moving."

Johnny was looking back at the slumped-over figure of Lon Shaw, and Clyde said, "You ride up front with me, Johnny."

As Clyde and Johnny began to ride Matt Daniels said, "I could go back and get his canteen and guns, Clyde."

Johnny looked quickly at Clyde, who caught his brother's look and said, "Leave 'em."

"We could use them, Clyde—"

"I said leave 'em! Let's move!"

As they started up again they all knew they were leaving a dead man behind. Matt Daniels was also thinking that a five-way split had just become a four-way split, which didn't bother him in the least.

Chapter Eight

When they camped that night Demi and Clint sat together while they ate. Before long Cal Ramsey joined them.

"What's the problem, Cal?" Clint asked before the deputy even spoke. He was able to read the expression on the man's face and knew he was unhappy about something.

Apparently it bothered Clyde that he wasn't being consulted enough to suit him. Clint was leading the posse, and Demi was doing the tracking, and that didn't leave him a whole hell of a lot to do. The least they could do was let him know what was going on once in a while. Of course, those weren't his exact words, but Clint knew that was what he meant. He also knew that the deputy was worried about looking bad in front of the rest of the posse, so he promised that in the future he would talk to him before they made a decision.

"This is just what I need," Clint said as Ramsey left them alone, "a deputy with his feelings hurt."

"Well, that's what happens when you're the great leader of a posse," Demi said, teasing him.

"You're a big help. Maybe I should let you go over and soothe his feelings."

She put her hand on his arm and said, "I'd much rather soothe yours."

"Go to sleep, you brazen hussy."

* * *

34

The following morning they found the dead man.

He was lying on his stomach and there was a bloody hole in his lower back on the right side.

"Yeah, I'd say you hit him, all right," Demi said to Clint.

"Ramsey, you want to check him and see if he's carrying anything?"

"Like what?"

"Like some of the money from the bank job."

"Oh, sure."

While Ramsey dismounted and checked the body, Clint and Demi searched the horizon for any sign of the man's horse. The big Swede, Olle, came up and said the others were curious about what was happening.

"Found a dead man, Olle," Demi said, "and we're just checking to see if we can tell whether or not he was one of the bank robbers."

"He ain't got any money on him at all," Ramsey said. He had turned the body over on its back during his search and both Clint and Demi looked at the dead man's face.

"Face mean anything to you?" Clint asked Demi and Ramsey.

"Not to me," Demi said. "What about you, Cal?"

Ramsey made a show of studying the man's face and said, "Can't say that I've ever seen him in town."

"What about on a wanted poster?" Clint asked.

Again Ramsey looked down, shook his head and said, "Not that I can recall."

"Olle?" Clint said.

"I haf never seen him in my shop."

"Then the only way we can tie him to the robbery is by that hole in his back."

"How's that?" Ramsey asked.

"I knew I hit one of those men as they were riding away," Clint explained. "This man could have been shot by anyone, but then again, he could be the one I hit. If we figure that way, then we know we're on the right trail."

"And the sheriff's chasing his tail," Demi said.

"He'll catch up when he figures it out. We'll keep on going. Mount up, Cal."

"Wait a minute," Ramsey said. He seemed to feel he had to dispute the point on behalf of the absent sheriff. "How can we be sure that's your bullet in him?"

"We can't, Cal," Clint said, still trying to cultivate some patience, "but unless you want to dig it out and compare it with mine, that's the assumption we're going to go under."

Ramsey didn't work up any further argument, although he seemed to want to, so with a last look down at the dead man he walked to his horse and mounted up.

"Olle," Clint said, "you can tell the rest of the men that we've found one of the bank robbers dead, and that leaves four to go. Okay?"

"*Ja*, I tell them."

"Trying to keep up morale?" Demi asked.

"It's an important part of keeping a posse together," Clint said. "Let them think they're accomplishing something and they'll stay happy. Make them think they're wasting their time, and you'll lose them."

"I don't think you should lie to them," Cal Ramsey said sullenly.

"I'm not." Clint turned in his saddle to face the deputy. "I believe that this man was one of the bank robbers, and that's what I'm telling them. I'm in charge of this posse, Cal, and I don't want anyone spreading dissension. They'll be told what I want them to be told. You got that?"

"Yeah," Ramsey said, even more sullen now, "I got it." He wheeled his horse around and rode back to the rest of the group.

Shaking her head, Demi looked at Clint and said, "Well, that's one posse member you sure kept happy."

The four men who rode into the town of Cornerstone, New Mexico were tired, hungry, and riding horses that weren't even fit for eating.

"We gonna stop and eat, Clyde?" Dan Clayton asked hopefully.

"We're gonna stop to store up on supplies, get us some fresh horses and get the hell out of here. By now they've found Lon, alive or dead, and either way they know they're on the right trail."

"Can't we take care of a few other needs while we're here?" Matt Daniels asked.

"You keep it in your pants, Matt. We don't need that kind of trouble now. Besides," Clyde said, looking around, "what the hell kind of woman you expect to find in this dust hole? More likely than not you'd end up catching something."

They pulled their horses up in front of the general store. Clyde said, "Johnny, you and Matt go and see if you can't get us some fresh horses. Dan, you and me are gonna get some supplies. Matt!"

"Yeah, Clyde?"

"Try not to kill anybody. Just get us some horses."

Three dead men later, the four men rode out of Cornerstone with fresh horses—though they weren't much better than the ones they had ridden in on—and a fresh store of supplies.

They were still tired.

Chapter Nine

When the posse rode into Cornerstone that night, the town—what there was of it—was still buzzing about what had happened earlier that day.

"Are we gonna spend the night here?" Cal Ramsey asked when they stopped at the livery stable.

"Yes, we are," Clint said. "We are also going to keep our ears open. Something happened in this town today, and I'd like to find out what without asking."

"That don't make sense," Ramsey complained.

"Believe me, kid, it does."

But Ramsey didn't believe him, as Clint found out a little later on.

They left Ramsey at the livery, to oversee the care and feeding of the horses, and went to the hotel to find accommodations for the members of the posse. Since Cornerstone was little more than a ghost town, there were rooms for everyone, and no one had to share.

"Any place around here to get something to eat?" Clint asked the elderly clerk.

"Café across the street," the old man said, "but I don't know how good the food will be. Ain't used to cooking for so many people."

"I guess we'll take our chances."

They stowed their gear in their rooms, and while most of

the posse stayed in their rooms to rest, Clint, Demi and Olle started across to the café.

They met up with Ramsey, and Clint told him to go to the general store and pick up supplies before he got something to eat. Ramsey didn't like it, but he did.

"Happier and happier," Demi said as Ramsey stalked over to the general store.

"I'm tired of babying him," Clint said.

"Be careful of that one," Olle Bjorkmn said. "He will take it for only so long, and then—*poof*!"

"I think he means—*boom*!" Demi said.

"Ramsey's got to learn," Clint said, although he was perfectly aware of the possibilities.

The café was empty, most of its tables covered with dust. A middle-aged woman came out from the back and cleaned off a table for them and then told them that she had beans and potatoes, potatoes and beans, or either one by itself.

"I'll try the beans and potatoes," Clint said.

"Me too," Demi said.

"*Ja*," Olle said.

"What did he say?"

"He said him too," Demi said, and the woman nodded and went to get their orders.

She was coming out of the kitchen with the three orders when they heard the shot, and Clint was the first one out the door. When the second shot came he pinpointed its source as the general store and headed for it at a dead run. The others were following behind.

When Clint reached the general store he found Cal Ramsey backed up against a wall by a woman and a boy, both with rifles. The woman was a hard forty or so, while the boy was in his late teens. Neither of them was holding his gun all that steady.

"What's going on here?" Clint demanded. Demi and Olle came rushing in after him, but he put his arms out to keep them from any unexpected actions that might prompt shooting.

"I don't know," Ramsey said. "These people just started firing at me."

"If I'd shot at him, he'd know it," the woman said. "Are you with him?"

"Yes, ma'am, we are."

At that the boy turned and pointed his rifle in their direction while the woman kept hers trained on Ramsey.

"Boy," Clint said, "you'd best point that gun somewhere else before I'm obliged to take it away from you."

The boy's nerve wavered for a moment and he looked over at his mother.

"What do you want here?" the woman asked, looking at Clint.

"I won't talk to you, ma'am, not while that boy is holding that gun on me. You can keep yours, but I'd prefer that he put his down, or else I'm going to take it from him."

The boy worked his hands nervously on the rifle, shifting his glance between Clint and his mother.

"He's either going to end up killing someone, or he's going to get hurt, ma'am," Clint said. "I really don't think you want it to be either way."

He gave her a few moments to work it out, and finally she said, "Put the rifle down, Jed."

"But, Ma—"

"Do as I say. Put it down."

The boy got a stubborn look on his face, but his mother's was even more stubborn, so he put the rifle down.

"Now," the woman said, "who are you?"

"Show her, Cal."

Cal frowned and said, "What?"

"Your badge, damn it."

"Oh, yeah." Ramsey opened his jacket and showed her the badge pinned to his shirt.

"Deputy?"

"Yes, ma'am," Clint said, "but not a very smart one, I'm afraid. We're part of a posse hunting five men who robbed a bank and killed a little girl in Phoenix, Texas."

"Five men?"

"Could be four by now," Clint said. "We found a dead man on the trail."

"Four then," she said. "They was here. Killed my man

and two men over to the livery. Took supplies and horses.''

"Why'd you shoot at this man?'' Clint asked, gesturing to Ramsey.

"He asked about what happened in town earlier,'' she said. "Said he was looking for some men. I thought he was friends with 'em.''

"Well, he's not, ma'am,'' Clint said, "and neither are we, so we'd be obliged if you'd put that gun down now.''

She looked at him, then nodded and lowered the gun.

"We're sorry for your loss, ma'am,'' Demi said.

"Sorry,'' the woman said dully.

"We'd like to buy some supplies, boy,'' Clint said. "Could you help us out on that?''

The boy looked at his mother, who nodded, and then he said, "Sure thing.''

"Just settle up with this gentleman here,'' Clint said, indicating Olle, "and the rest of us will go outside.''

Clint motioned for Ramsey to join him and Demi outside. "You had to ask,'' Clint said when Ramsey came out.

"I was just—''

"You were just being ornery, damn it,'' Clint said. "From now on you do as I say, Cal, or so help me I'll pin that badge to your ass. You got that?''

"Yeah, I got it.''

"We've got food waiting,'' Clint said to Demi. They started for the café, but Clint turned to face Ramsey again and said, "And for chrissake, if you're going to wear the badge, wear it where people can see it!''

Later that night Clint answered a knock at his door. "Do you mind?'' Demi asked when the door opened.

"Not if you don't.''

She entered, shut the door behind her and said, "You know I don't.''

After they made love the first time Demi stretched luxuriously in bed and said, "This is the only good part of this whole mess.''

"I guess it just proves that there's good in everything, if

you look hard enough.''

She moved her hand underneath the sheets and said, ''I'm looking.''

When she found what she was looking for she stroked it until it was hard and pulsing, and then she took it in her mouth. Just when Clint thought he wouldn't be able to hold back any longer she allowed him to pop free, only to climb up on him and capture him again, this time in a slick, seemingly endless sheath.

''You like being on top,'' he said.

''I love it,'' she said. She stared down at him and said, ''It means I'm in control.''

''Is that so?'' He took her by the shoulders and roughly changed places with her. When he was on top he began to take her in long hard strokes and she bit her lip to keep from screaming. When she came she lifted her hips, raising them both off the bed, and then when he began to fill her up she raked his back with her nails.

A few moments later, after she'd regained her breath, she said, ''I guess the bottom isn't so bad either, huh?''

Chapter Ten

Before moving out the next morning Clint asked some questions at the livery. The owner and his brother had been killed when they refused to give four horses to two men, someone told him.

"Two men?"

"Yes," the stablehand said. "The other two were at the general store. Charlie Bartlett didn't like their looks and when he heard the shots from here he pulled a rifle out. Those two shot him dead. After that they grabbed all the supplies they needed, plus the four horses, and lit out."

When Clint asked the man what kind of horses they had he found out that they weren't much better than fly bait.

"What about the horses they left behind?"

"They're out back. You want to buy them?"

"No, thanks, but I do want to look at them."

"Help yourself." If Clint didn't want to buy them the man wasn't interested in him anymore and left.

Demi went with Clint to look at the horses, and it was obvious even with a day's rest that the animals had been ridden hard.

"They know there's a posse on their tail that won't quit," Clint said.

"They know they killed Jenny," Demi said. "They know they killed a little girl. That's why they're pushing."

"The animals they took won't last long, not according to what we've just been told. This is our chance to really close some ground on them."

"Then let's move," she said.

When they returned to the livery the entire posse had their horses saddled. Clint and Demi mounted up and led them out of town. With a little luck, they'd catch up to them by nightfall.

"Horses," Matt Daniels said.

They were on a rise looking down at a ranch house and a corral with about a half a dozen horses in it.

"Good ones too," Dan Clayton said.

"Do we take them?" Daniels asked, looking at Clyde.

They'd had a confrontation following the incident in Cornerstone, and Daniels had backed down only because Johnny Hogan and Dan Clayton would have backed Clyde at that point. However, Daniels felt sooner or later he'd be able to get Clayton over to his side, and then they'd be able to take Clyde. The kid wouldn't be a problem, then, not after Clyde was gone.

Now Daniels was "asking" Clyde what they should do.

"We need horses, Clyde," Johnny said.

"I know it!" Clyde snapped. Thanks to Daniels's quick trigger finger in Cornerstone, Clyde couldn't afford to do things the easy way. It would take too long.

"We need the horses," he said, "and we'll take them any way we can."

Even that, in some small way, was a victory for Matt Daniels over Clyde Hogan.

"What are we gonna do, Sheriff?" Sam Dodger asked Sheriff John Russell.

They were in Mexico and there was still no sign of the five men. It was time to give it up—past time, Russell knew—and try to catch up with the others.

"We're going back," Russell said.

Dodger looked at Willie Akens, and the same thought was on both of their minds.

It was about time.

Chapter Eleven

It was past midday when Clint, Demi and the rest of their party came upon the ranch house where the Hogan gang had gotten fresh mounts. They found that the gang had left mistrust and carnage in their wake.

"What do you want?" a woman with a gun asked them from the window of the house.

Clint told Cal Ramsey to do the talking, since he was the one with the badge.

"Ma'am, I'm a deputy sheriff from the town of Phoenix. We're a-hunting four or five men who robbed a bank there and killed a little girl."

"Get down off your horse so's I can see yore badge," the woman called.

Ramsey did as she asked and stood so she could see his tin star.

"Come ahead, but just you," she said then.

Ramsey looked back at Clint, who nodded, and then the deputy entered the house. He came out a few moments later and approached Clint and Demi.

"They were here. They pistol-whipped her man and took four horses."

"Is he dead?" Clint asked.

"No, but he's banged up pretty bad."

"Let me have a look," Demi said, dismounting.

Clint told the rest of the posse to water their horses, then dismounted himself and followed Demi and Ramsey into the house.

The couple's name was Norton, and Mr. Norton was lying on a bed, his face a mass of cuts and swollen bruises. Demi tried to have a look, but Mrs. Norton seemed leery of letting another woman near her husband, even in his present condition. Not wanting to rattle the woman any more than she already was, Demi backed off.

Clint told the woman that they would be on their way as soon as they watered their horses and then asked her if she could tell them what direction the men went in.

"I shore can," she said. "I watched them bastids leave and they headed west. Mister, if you can get us our horses back, we'd be much obliged."

"We'll either get your horses or their worth, Mrs. Norton. We're sorry for your trouble, but thank you for the information."

"You get them bastids, mister!" the woman shouted as Clint left the house. "You get them and you string them up high!"

"We'll do what has to be done, ma'am," Clint said and left the house. Demi had already watered his mount and handed him the reins.

"According to Mrs. Norton they've got themselves some good horses now," he said to Demi. "Young and fresh and, if we can judge from the others in the corral, damn fine stock. We're closing on them, but it won't be easy from here on in. Their animals are fresher than ours."

"I guess that means we need some fresh horses ourselves," Demi said.

"We'll look into it in the next town," Clint said. "I don't think these people are ready to talk about selling any of their remaining animals."

Clint called for the posse to mount up and then he and Demi rode to the front and led the way west.

"Time to split up," Clyde Hogan said.

"What?" Matt Daniels was surprised. This was not an expected development.

"We'll be harder to track and find if we split up," Clyde said. "It's the only thing that makes sense."

"Sure," Daniels said, "if I've got my share of the money it makes sense."

"I told you we ain't splittin' that money up until we reach Inferno."

"Inferno," Daniels said, almost spitting the word out. "Who'd name a town such a thing. Why do we have to wait until we get there?"

"Because we agreed," Clyde said, his eyes boring into Daniels's. He knew that Daniels had plans of his own, but Daniels would get his way over Clyde Hogan's dead body.

"You got any objections, let's get them out of the way now, Matt, because we got to get moving."

"I just want my money, Clyde, that's all. I don't like being so far from it."

"All right then," Clyde said, "you ride with me and we'll let Johnny and Dan ride together. How's that?"

"We keep the money with us?"

"That's right."

Daniels turned to Dan Clayton and asked, "How do you feel about that, Dan?"

"I don't like being so far from my money, either," Clayton said, "but I don't guess Clyde's gonna run out on his own brother. I'll go along with it."

"All right," Clyde said. "Now that that's settled let's get a move on. Johnny, you know which way to go. Swing south for a while, then cut back west and head for Inferno. We'll be there waiting for you."

"Good luck, Clyde."

"Watch yourself, kid."

Clyde watched as Johnny and Dan rode south, then turned to Daniels and said, "Let's move, Matt. We got a ways to go, yet."

"Want me to carry all of the money, Clyde?"

"That's okay, Matt," Clyde said. "It ain't no hardship for me to carry half."

"Just trying to be helpful."

Yeah, Clyde thought, *I'll bet you are*. Matt Daniels did not have a helpful or friendly bone in his body, and Clyde Hogan knew that before this thing was over one of them was going to be dead.

He and Daniels were the only two of the gang who had ever pulled a bank job before Phoenix, and they had both wanted to be inside the bank. The other three were all inexperienced, which showed when Lon Shaw disobeyed orders. He was supposed to stay outside with the horses but had panicked and run into the bank just moments before the shooting had started. In fact, his rushing in that way had *started* the goddamned shooting, although Daniels was the first one to fire.

Shaw was dead now and probably deserved to be as far as Clyde was concerned. The one Clyde worried about was Johnny, who had never done anything unlawful until Clyde brought him in on this job. Clyde himself had recruited Clayton, although the two didn't know each other all that well, and Johnny had brought Shaw into it. Needing at least one experienced hand, Clyde had overruled all his own objections and brought Matt Daniels in, even though he knew that Daniels's quick temper and even quicker trigger finger could bring trouble—as it had in Cornerstone.

All Clyde Hogan cared about was him and Johnny coming out of this with a stake. He didn't want Johnny to have to hold up another bank, and if Matt Daniels thought he was going to do anything to foul up Clyde's plans, then he was a dead man.

"They've split up," Demi said. She had dismounted in order to check the ground carefully for sign, and had no doubt now that the four men had split up. "Two south and two west."

She looked up at Clint, who muttered, "Shit."

The posse's force had already been cut in half by separating once; now they'd have to do it again—but they wouldn't need to halve their force again.

"All right, here's the way it's going to be," Clint said, addressing the rest of the posse. "Six of us are going to keep going west. The other two will camp here and wait for the sheriff to catch up. When he does, tell him to head south and track the other two.''

''Who stays behind?'' Ramsey asked.

Clint needed to leave someone he could trust behind, but he didn't want to leave Demi, so he chose the big Swede.

''Olle, pick another man and wait here for the sheriff. Okay?''

''*Ja*, I do it,'' Olle said. He turned and called to one of the other men, who nodded.

''All right,'' Clint said, ''let's get moving. Olle, wait at least a day and then follow the trail of the second two men south.''

''I don't read the ground so good as Demi,'' the Swede said.

''No problem,'' Clint assured him. ''Just keep heading south and see what you can find.''

''*Ja*, I do. Good luck to you.''

''And to you,'' Clint said, and continued west with a posse that was now reduced to six.

Chapter Twelve

The first town Clint, Demi and the others hit was called Joryville. It was getting near dark, and although Clint was tempted to keep riding, he decided to stop. The others weren't used to all the riding that they were doing and were pretty tired as were their mounts.

At one point Clint entertained the idea of leaving them all behind and tracking the two men himself. The quicker he got this over with, the faster he could get back to living his life. He put the idea aside for the moment but did not discard it altogether.

When they reached Joryville he instructed a couple of the other possemen to see to the horses, and he, Ramsey and Demi paid a call on the sheriff.

After Ramsey identified himself the sheriff introduced himself as Dave Riddle.

"Sheriff, we've been trailing five men for a couple of days now," Clint explained. "We found one dead on the trail, and the other four split into pairs. We tracked two of them this far. Have you had any strangers in town today?"

"Let me think," Riddle said, scratching the back of his head. While he thought his eyes roamed over Demi, who endured the examination quietly. Riddle was a tall, lanky man in his late thirties with a remarkably homely face, and it was obvious that most of his pleasure with women came from looking.

"I think we had a couple of strangers come through town."

"Through?" Clint asked. "They didn't stop?"

"I don't know."

"Sheriff, don't you make it your business to keep track of strangers in your town?"

"You tryin' to tell me my job, mister?" Riddle demanded. "Are you a lawman?"

"No, I'm just riding with the posse."

"Well, if you ain't a lawman you ain't got no right to criticize one. Who are you, anyhow?"

"My name's Adams, Sheriff, Clint Adams."

The sheriff frowned for a moment, and then realization flooded his face. His eyes widened and his Adam's apple bobbed a few times before he found his voice. "Adams? The one they call the Gunsmith?"

"I guess."

"I didn't mean nothing, Mr. Adams," he blustered. "I mean, by what I said—"

"Sheriff, we'll be in town overnight. While we're here, I'll be checking for those two strangers you think you saw. If something happens, you'll know why."

"Yes, sir, I surely will. You can count on my help."

Clint looked away from the lawman in disgust and said to the others, "Let's go. I need a drink."

They walked to the saloon in silence and found the other three men waiting there.

"Who wants to go over to the hotel and book our rooms?" Clint asked, knowing he'd have at least a couple of takers.

"I'll go," a man named Granger said. "I'm beat, anyway."

"I'll go too," a man named Stevens said. "If I have a second drink I'll fall asleep right here."

Both men were shopkeepers and were beginning to show the wear of two days riding with a posse.

"All right. We'll be along later."

Both men nodded and left the saloon. The remaining man, Fleming, seemed more used to life in the saddle.

"I think I'll play some cards," he said, eyeing a game going on at a table.

"Don't play too late," Clint warned him. "We'll be getting an early start."

"Don't worry," Fleming said, "I'll be ready."

Clint, Demi and Ramsey stepped up to the bar and ordered beer.

"That sheriff was sure afraid of you," Ramsey said, looking at Clint with renewed respect.

"He's a fool and incompetent," Clint said. "I can't stand an incompetent lawman."

At that remark Cal Ramsey seemed a little uneasy, probably wondering if the Gunsmith considered him incompetent. He finished his beer and said, "I think I'll go over to the hotel. See you in the morning."

"Fine."

"You want me to check if two strangers registered?"

Clint looked at him quickly and said, "No!" He realized he'd said it too sharply and tried to modify it. "No, that's all right. I'll check around before I turn in."

"And if you find them?"

"I'll come and get you before I brace them. Go on, turn in."

"All right," Ramsey said, and left the saloon.

Clint and Demi sipped their beers in silence for a while. Demi was thinking about the way the sheriff had reacted when he heard Clint's name. She was impressed but puzzled by Clint's reaction. Ever since that moment he seemed to be carrying a dark cloud around with him.

"You don't like being called that, do you?"

"What?" he asked absently, looking into his beer.

"The Gunsmith."

She saw him make a face and said, "I wish I could find the newspaperman who first stuck that label on me."

"How long ago?"

"A long time," he said, "a great long time."

"Did you ever think about changing your name? You didn't have to tell the sheriff that you were Clint Adams. You could have told him your name was Smith or Jones.''

"No, I couldn't."

"Why not?"

"Because that's my name. I'm Clint Adams, not . . . the Gunsmith. I'm Clint Adams, and I won't deny that. I'm not ashamed of who I am, Demi."

"Of what they call you, then?"

"If I was what they all think I was, then I'd be ashamed no matter what they called me."

He turned to the bartender and said, "Another beer." He looked at Demi, but she shook her head. She still had half of her first one.

When the bartender came with the beer, Clint asked, "Have you seen two strangers today?"

"I just seen six."

"Before us, I mean."

The bartender was a rotund man in his late fifties, and he'd logged a lot of time behind bars just like this one. "They on the dodge?"

"Yes."

"What'd they do?"

"Robbed a bank, rode over a little girl while they were escaping."

"A little girl? How old?"

Clint looked at Demi who said, "Seven. She was my niece."

"Was?"

"She's dead."

The bartender hesitated only a moment before saying, "They're at the hotel."

"Thanks." Clint turned to Demi and said, "Let's go."

Out on the street it had grown dark and Demi said, "They're in the hotel, and so is the posse. That's ironic."

"They had to rest sometime. They must have thought they'd shaken us by splitting up."

"Are you going to wake the others?"

"No," he said. "I don't want anybody getting killed." He looked at her and said, "I want you to stay down here."

"Oh no, no way," she said firmly, shaking her head. "I can handle myself—"

"I know you can," he said, interrupting her, "or I wouldn't be leaving you down here. I need you here in case they get by me."

She thought it over and, as he had hoped, bought it.

"All right."

"I'll call out when I've got them."

She nodded, and he went into the hotel.

"Two men checked in earlier today," he said to the dapper desk clerk. "What room are they in?"

"I can't—"

"Mister, I can go over and get the sheriff so you can tell him, but I haven't got time to do that. What room are they in?"

"Room twelve, on the second floor."

Clint went up the steps to the second floor and crept along the hall until he located room twelve. He put his ear to the door first, and when he didn't hear anything he backed up, drew his gun and kicked the door in.

He leaped into the room, staying low, with his gun held out in front of him at the ready, but there was no need. If there had been two men there, there was only one now.

He walked to the window, opened it and called out to Demi to come on up. When she got there they were joined by the other posse members, who had responded to the noise of the door being kicked open.

"They're gone," Clint said.

Demi looked down at the dead man on the floor and said, "Who's—"

"He tried to brace them alone, even after I told him not to." Clint turned the dead man over onto his back so they could all see who he was. "They knifed him," Clint said, looking down at the body of Deputy Cal Ramsey, "nice and quiet, with the posse sleeping all around them."

Chapter Thirteen

After the body had been removed, Clint met with the posse in the largest of the hotel rooms that they'd taken.

"We'll have to go after them tonight," he said.

"In the dark?" Granger asked.

"We can't afford to let them get a night's ride on us," Clint explained.

"Yeah, but we could get killed riding around out there in the dark," Stevens spoke up.

"Look, I'm not asking anyone who doesn't want to to come with me," Clint said, "But I'm leaving tonight. I won't hold any hard feelings against anyone who doesn't want to come."

Granger and Stevens looked at each other and Stevens said, "It's just that Granger and me ain't used to this, Adams. We can't be away from our businesses so long, and—"

"All right, you can head back home in the morning," Clint said, dismissing both men. He turned to Fleming. "What about you?"

"I'd like to help out, I really would," Fleming said, "but the odds don't look so good anymore, you know?"

"The sheriff will be coming along any time now," Demi said.

"Well, I'll tell you what I'll do," Fleming said. "I'll just wait here for him to catch up, and when he does I'll bring him along."

Demi looked at them all, but before she could speak Clint turned and walked out.

"He's too good a man to tell you what you are," she said to the three men. "I'd tell you, bit I ain't got the time to waste." She ran out of the room after Clint and caught up to him on the steps.

"I'm going with you," she said.

He looked at her, and then said, "I figured you would. Can I talk you out of it?"

"Hell, no."

"Let's go talk to the sheriff, then."

"What about?"

"He'll have to take care of Ramsey's body while we're gone."

The sheriff had another problem too. "His badge—what do I do with it?"

"Hold on to it," Clint said. "The sheriff of Phoenix should be along any time now."

"Maybe you should take it and wear it if you're going after those two," Riddle said.

"No."

"You used to be a lawman, didn't you?"

"Used to be," Clint said. "Now I'm just a private citizen doing some posse work, that's all."

"Oh, give it to me," Demi said then, reaching for the tin star. "I'll wear it. Somebody's got to be able to show a star, and we were all sworn in before we left. I guess that gives me the right to wear it, don't it?"

"I guess it does," Riddle said, looking at Clint.

"Why not?" Clint said. "Sheriff, we're riding out tonight. Would you take care of the deputy's body?"

"It's over to the undertaker's now," Riddle said. "If that sheriff of yours comes in, I'll tell him where it is."

"Thanks."

Outside the office Demi paused to pin on the badge, then asked Clint, "How's it look?"

"Fine," he said, "it looks fine. Just like a big bull's-eye on your chest."

"That's encouraging."

"Let's get to the livery, Demi. We've got some hard riding to do."

"What about supplies?"

"We'll have to pick up what we need in the next town. I don't want those jaspers getting too far ahead of us. They killed a little girl, and now they've killed a deputy. It's about time somebody stopped them."

When Demi saw the look in the Gunsmith's eyes she almost felt sorry for those men.

"Daniels," Clyde Hogan said when he and Matt Daniels had put some miles between them and the town, "you have got the lamest excuse for brains I ever came across."

"What do you want to go and say that for?"

"You got the drop on that badge-toter fair and square," Clyde said. "What did you have to go and kill him for?"

"He had the drop on *us* didn't he? What'd you think he was going to do, kiss ya?"

"He wasn't gonna kill us. You could of knocked him out instead of putting that pig-sticker into him."

"Then he would have woke up and got on our trail again."

"Yeah, well now not only did we rob a bank and kill a little girl, now we killed a lawman, thanks to you."

"And your brother killed the little girl!" Daniels said defiantly. "It don't matter why that posse is after us, Clyde, because they're after us, and that's what counts."

"Let's get moving again," Clyde said, realizing that he wasn't getting through to the other man.

The thing that was really worrying Clyde Hogan was that he hadn't known that Matt Daniels even carried a knife until he shoved it into that deputy's stomach.

What other surprises did the man have up his sleeve?

Chapter Fourteen

It was almost morning when Clint and Demi came within sight of the next town. The signpost said it was called Hangtown.

"Why would they call it that?" Demi wondered aloud.

"Why call a town anything?" Clint replied. "It's just a town. I once knew a town called Hangtown. *They* called it that because they hung a man once a day."

"How terrible."

"It sure was," Clint said. "That man had a mighty long neck before they were through."

She frowned a moment before she realized he'd made a joke and then laughed dryly. Her stomach chose that moment to make its emptiness known, and she put her hand on it to quiet it down.

"I'm hungry too," he assured her. "We'll get something in town, stock up on supplies, and keep on going . . . that is, if you're up to it."

"As long as the alternative is to let you go on alone, I'm up to it."

"You're a credit to your badge," he said teasingly, but he meant it. He hadn't known many men with her courage or dedication.

When they rode into town they hitched up in front of the general store and went in to buy supplies.

As they were putting the supplies away in their saddlebags Demi asked, "Should we ask the local law if any strangers rode in?"

"I doubt that they rode in or through," he said. "Most likely they bypassed this town altogether to get to the next one way before we did."

"So now that we have supplies, we'll bypass the next one to make up the time?"

"Right, and since there's only two of us, and I'm fairly certain *we* won't get lost, we'll keep riding at night."

"Can we get that something to eat now?"

"We already did," he said, handing her a piece of hardtack.

"This ain't exactly what my stomach had in mind," she said, "but I guess it'll have to do." She took a bite and began to chew vigorously while mounting up.

Two days later Demi crouched down to examine the ground and exclaimed in disgust, "We aren't gaining on them at all!"

"Are we losing ground?"

"No, but—"

"Then we're doing fine."

She stood up and looked at Clint, and he could see the strain on her face. He knew what she was going to ask before she asked it, and he didn't blame her one bit. It takes a special kind of temperament to have the patience to hunt a man.

"Clint, how long will you look for them?"

"Until I find them."

"Why? You're only here because my sister shamed you into it. Jenny didn't mean anything to you."

"There's Ramsey."

"He didn't mean anything to you either."

"He was a lawman," Clint said. "You don't kill a lawman."

Demi studied him for a few moments and guessed that it was hard to get the badge out of your blood when you'd worn it as long as he had.

"What about you?" Clint asked. "How long are you willing to go on looking?"

"I'm tired, I won't deny that, but I'll keep going as long as it takes. I couldn't face my sister if I didn't, and I loved Jenny too much not to." She hesitated a moment and then added, "It helps that you're along too."

"That's how I feel."

He stepped forward and they touched their dried lips to each other's. She laid her head against his chest and he could feel the weariness inside of her, the kind that gets into your bones.

"You're doing fine, you know," he said. "If it wasn't for you we would have lost them long ago."

"I'm doing the best I can."

"That's pretty damn good, if you ask me."

She looked up at him and said, "I guess we better get going, huh? What I wouldn't give for a nice hotel room with a soft bed where we could—"

"Later," he said. "Let's don't talk about that now, because this ground is too hard for me to do to you what I have in mind."

"Is that a threat or a promise?"

"You'll find out."

"You reckon they're still on our trail after all this time, Clyde?"

"I know they are. I can feel them." Clyde looked behind them. "I can almost see them, and I know I feel their breath down my back. They ain't gonna give up, Matt."

"Maybe we ought to split up again."

Clyde knew what Daniels had in mind. If they split up, each carrying half the money, he'd take off with his half and never look back, because a half was a hell of a lot better than what had started out to be a fifth.

"No, that's okay, Matt," Clyde said. "We'll stay together until we meet Johnny and Dan in Inferno."

"We're less than a day's ride from there now," Daniels said. "We gonna lead them right there? Right to Inferno?"

"If they come into that town after us," Clyde said, "They'll deserve whatever they get. Come on."

"Damn it!"

The epithet was so violent that Demi reined in her horse and stared at Clint's back as he rode by her. He stopped then and turned to face her.

"What is it?" she asked.

"I just got it."

"Got what?"

"I just figured out where they're going, and I am good and goddamned mad at myself for not having seen it sooner."

"Where?"

"How could I have known, though?" Clint went on, as if he hadn't heard her. "I always thought it was a myth, a legend."

"What? What are you talking about?"

"Inferno," he said. "I'm talking about Inferno."

"What's that?"

"It's a town I've heard about for a lot of years, but I always thought it was just a story."

"Why? What kind of town is it?"

"It's an outlaw town. A town inhabited totally by men who are on the run, who have a price on their head. They're supposed to have a mayor, a sheriff—everything a regular town has—but all the positions are held by wanted men."

"And you think that's where they're headed."

"The general location seems right, but it's hard to find. No lawman has ever found it."

"Well," she said, looking down at the badge on her chest, "it looks like a lawwoman is going to be the first to do it."

"Yeah, it looks that way," he said thoughtfully. He was trying to think of a way to get her out of it now, because if the town of Inferno really did exist, she was going to have to do a lot more than just handle herself with a gun.

A hell of a lot more.

Chapter Fifteen

The mayor of Inferno was Mike Hedge, and his hand-picked sheriff was Hank Meade. Combined, the price on their heads was over two thousand dollars the last time either of them heard.

"What's the word on that bank job Clyde Hogan was supposed to pull?" Hedge asked Meade.

"Word is he pulled it off all right, but killed a little girl while escaping."

"Hogan did?"

"Or one of his gang. I hear there's a posse hot on their tail."

"Well, as long as they show up with the money we'll have to let them stay. And if that posse shows up, we'll just have to take care of it. Maybe you'd better put on a few more deputies just to be on the safe side."

"Right."

"What else is on the agenda?" Hedge asked.

"The Gatling boys are two weeks behind on their payments."

"Give them a day to pay up, and then kick them out. I'm sure there are a few posses and bounty hunters out there looking for them. Is that it?"

"That's it, Mike."

"Okay then, I'll see you later at the saloon."

This was one of Hedge and Meade's weekly meetings to

discuss the operations of Inferno. The town was a sanctuary for any desperado who could afford the price. The initial buy-in was ten percent of your last job, and thereafter you paid twenty-five dollars a week, in addition to your hotel fees and your meals. Anyone who fell behind on his payments was run out of town and could only get back in with another ten percent buy-in fee. This was the way Inferno had been run for the twenty years or so it had been in existence, and Mike Hedge—Inferno's fourth mayor—had no intention of changing it.

Nobody really knew the whole story behind Inferno—who founded it and who opened it up to wanted men—but most of the men who came there were simply satisfied that there was someplace for them to go, even if it was expensive.

Forty-five years old, Hedge had been mayor of Inferno for five years, and in all that time there had been very few problems that he and Meade had not been able to handle. Now Hogan was heading this way with a posse on his tail, and his saddlebags full of money. Would the one offset the other?

He hoped so.

Meade went right to the saloon. He was thirty-eight, and until he'd become Hedge's sheriff he'd been nothing but a bank and train robber, with a price on his head. He guessed there was probably still a price on his head, but he couldn't imagine ever leaving Inferno, and that, he thought, would have been the only time he would have had to worry about things like bounty hunters and posses.

Until now.

During the years he had been sheriff of Inferno all he'd ever had to deal with were drunks, men like the Gatlings who dropped behind in their dues, and gambling disputes. A lot of men had come to Inferno while on the dodge, but none had ever come close to leading a posse there. In fact, in all the years that the town had been in existence no posse or lawman had ever set foot in the town.

Keeping things that way was now in the hands of Hank

Meade, and the possibilities did not escape the sheriff's notice.

In the near future, his name could become as big a legend as Inferno itself.

"That's it?" Matt Daniels asked.

They had topped a rise, and suddenly, as if by magic, there was a town in front of them. It was as if someone had dug out a long, shallow hole and put down a town in it.

"That's Inferno," Clyde said.

"How do you know?" Daniels suddenly asked, frowning at the man who hated to be called Hammerhead Hogan. "You led us straight here as if you been here before."

"I have," Clyde Hogan said. "And now I'm back."

And there might be some people, he knew, who wouldn't be happy about that.

"Let's go, Matt," Clyde said. "There are some people I've been waiting a long time to see."

Clyde Hogan remembered Mike Hedge and Hank Meade very well, and he was sure they remembered him—although he wasn't the same young man they remembered. He wasn't "young Hammerhead" anymore, and he hoped that neither one of them would call him that when they saw him, because he didn't want to have to kill them.

Not right away, anyway.

"It's gone," Demi said.

"What do you mean it's gone?" Clint asked, looking down at her. "How can a trail just disappear? You've been following it for days on end—"

"It just . . . disappeared."

Looking annoyed, Clint dismounted and together they looked out over the rocky terrain ahead of them.

"It's out there, Demi," Clint said. "Inferno. It's out there somewhere. It's just like the stories say."

"What do the stories say, Clint?"

"That the land around Inferno won't hold sign. That when you get close, the ground just swallows it up."

"That's ridiculous."

"Then where did the sign go?"

"It's got to be here . . . somewhere," she said, gesturing helplessly.

"Yeah, sure." He put his fists on his hips and stared intently ahead.

"What should we do?"

For a moment she thought that maybe he didn't hear her, but then he shook his head slightly and said, "Oh, I guess we'll go back to the last town we passed through and start looking again in the morning."

"Without a trail to follow—"

"If Inferno is out there," he said, interrupting her, "I'll find it. Don't worry. You've taken us this far, now I'll take us the rest of the way."

"What makes you think you can find it?"

"An old lawman instinct I've never been able to shake," he said, confiding in her. "It's out there. I can feel it!"

Chapter Sixteen

The first time through the town called Driftwood, they had not even stopped for supplies. They had watered their horses, had a drink each and then left again. Now that they were back they dropped their horses off at the livery and walked to the saloon.

"What about the hotel?"

"We'll get a room later," he said. "Let's wash away some dust first."

"I could use a bath."

"You'll get that too."

There was something eating at him, Demi knew, and she was pretty damn sure that the something was called Inferno.

In the saloon they each ordered a beer and Clint sidestepped the bartender's natural attempt to find something out about strangers.

"I came here to drink, friend," he said, "not to answer a lot of fool questions."

"Sorry, mister," the bartender said. "I didn't mean nothing—"

"If you don't mean nothing you shouldn't talk," Clint said, cutting the man off. "In the future, don't talk unless you do mean something."

"Sure, mister, sure."

When the bartender fled to the other end of the bar Demi said to Clint, "Can we take a table and talk?"

"Sure, why not?"

The place was fairly empty, in spite of the late hour, and they had their pick of tables, but Clint selected one in a corner from which he could watch the entire room with his back to the wall.

"What's going on?" Demi asked as they sat down. She kept her voice down so that only Clint could hear her.

"What do you mean?"

"Don't be cute with me, Mr. Clint Adams. You're up to something, and something's eating at you. We're in this together and I want to know what's going on."

Clint paused, as though turning something over in his mind. "I'm going into Inferno—"

"Alone?" she asked, interrupting him. "Are you crazy? You used to be a lawman. If you go into that town alone, they'll tear you to pieces."

"That's just it. I'm not going in as Clint Adams, ex-lawman. I'm going to go in as Clint Adams, the Gunsmith."

She stared at him for a moment, then shook her head. "Now you're confusing me. You hate that name, but you're gonna go into that town and announce yourself?"

"There are several other names I could try to use," he said. "Warren Murphy and Bill Wallmann to name a couple, but somebody in that town might recognize me. If I get caught in a lie right off, I'm committing suicide."

"You're doing that anyway!"

"No, I'm not. Listen to me," he said, hitching his chair up closer to the table. "Every lawman worth his salt would give his eyeteeth to find Inferno."

"If it exists."

"It exists, all right. Everybody knows it, but nobody ever talks about it. It's a legend, and legends are feared and revered."

"You ought to know," she commented, and then kept her eyes on him to see if he got angry. When he didn't she knew she wasn't going to be able to talk him out of it.

"For once in my life I'll use my reputation to my advantage, and possibly put an end to Inferno once and for all."

"Why? Why this sudden urge to put an end to Inferno?"

"Demi, this is like . . . like finding Atlantis."

She was educated; he figured she'd understand the comparison, and she did. "Come on—"

"It's true. Say the name *Inferno* to any lawman and he gets a faraway look. Say it to a bounty hunter and you can see the dollar signs in his eyes. It's been years since I was a lawman, but when I realized where we were headed it was like I'd never taken the badge off. It's very hard to explain, but it's like no other feeling in the world."

"Is that a fact?" she asked. "Why don't we go over to the hotel and take a room and I'll try and give you a feeling to compare it with."

Clint was so pumped up with adrenaline that the idea of going to bed with Demi at that moment was even more appealing than usual. It might be a good idea, he was thinking, to work some of the feeling off with her and then think over his plan carefully and rationally.

"All right," he said to her surprise, "you're on."

"My God!" Demi cried out.

Clint was on top of her, her buttocks cupped in his hands, and he was plowing into her like he wanted to go right through. She'd had intentions of giving *him* some feelings to use for comparison, but it was working out the other way around. She had never felt so much pent-up energy in a man before, and although it was more exciting than anything she had ever felt before, it also frightened her. She looked up into his face once and the expression there made her wonder if she even existed for him at that moment.

"I've never . . ." she said, trying to get her breath back, "experienced . . . anything like that . . . before in . . . my life."

Now that he was more relaxed, Clint felt slightly guilty for having used her that way. "I'm sorry," he said.

"Clint, it was wonderful, but it was also . . . frightening.

I felt as if I wasn't even here in the room for you. Your mind was just off somewhere else . . . probably in Inferno.''

"I know," he said.

"This is like a fever, isn't it?"

She had described it perfectly, and he nodded. "That's it exactly, Demi. It's a fever, and no lawman, ex-lawman, bounty hunter or anyone else connected with law enforcement could resist it if he were in my place. I've got to go into that town!"

"And get out alive," she added, "or hadn't you thought that far ahead?"

"I'm going to get in and get out with the man who killed Jenny and Cal Ramsey."

"You sound very sure of yourself, Clint, or is that a symptom of the fever?"

"Demi, you've got to stay behind when I go in."

"When you go in? You keep talking about going in—you've got to find the damned place first!"

"I told you, I'll find it."

"All right, let's say you do find it. Why do I have to stay behind? Because I'm a woman? Because you don't want me to get hurt? Because I might get in your way? Come on, tell me the truth. Why can't I go?"

"Because," he said, "if I can't get out, I'm going to need someone on the outside to get me out."

"Damn you, Clint Adams." He had come up with the one reason she'd go for.

Still later he explained to her his behavior in the saloon, when he'd snapped at the bartender.

"There are times that I really do feel that way, but that wasn't one of them."

"Why did you do it, then?"

"This town is real close to Inferno, Demi," he explained. "My guess is that the bartender is sort of a spotter for them."

"What makes you say that?"

"If you wanted somebody to report to you on all strangers who came to town, who would you pick?"

She nodded and said, "A bartender."

"Every time. At one time or another almost every stranger will show up at the town saloon."

"So you wanted to show the bartender that you were a nasty hardcase."

"It wouldn't hurt to be thought of that way."

"But he doesn't know who you are."

"That's all right, he can describe me. That's another thing that a bartender develops, a good eye for descriptions. When a bartender tells you what a man looks like, you might as well be looking at a tintype."

"I still think this is a crazy idea."

"You got another one?"

"Yeah. Wait for John Russell to show up. If what you say is true, he'll be just as feverish about getting to Inferno as you are, but at least he'll have the posse with him."

"Or what's left of it. No, if I wait for Russell and the posse, a lot of people will get killed. What I've got to do is go into Inferno and come out with a killer—and the town's location."

"Then what?"

"Then I'll notify the governor and he can send the professionals in to clean up Inferno." He put his hands behind his head and stared at the ceiling. "I tell you, a lot of flyers are going to be torn up when that town falls."

"Have you considered something?"

"What?"

"If this works," she said, "if you engineer the destruction of Inferno, you'll make the Gunsmith an even bigger legend than he already is."

Clint frowned as he realized the truth behind her words. He pondered that for a moment, then said, "I've got that solved."

"I was afraid you'd say that."

"I'll just have to make sure that someone else gets the credit."

"Like who? Russell?"

That idea didn't appeal to him. Helping Russell become a

legend wouldn't give him any pleasure at all. "I'll think of somebody. By the time this is finished, I'll think of some-one."

"Or be dead."

"Well, look on the bright side."

"What bright side?"

"If I'm dead, I won't have to think of someone."

Chapter Seventeen

Clyde Hogan and Matt Daniels had ridden into Inferno well before dark, but it wasn't until after the curtain of night had fallen that they were allowed in to see Mayor Hedge.

"I remember you," Hedge said to Hogan. Hogan remained silent and stared at the mayor. The man had grown fat and complacent and looked older than he was. Meade, on the other hand, seemed to have grown harder during the three years since they'd last seen each other.

"Yeah, I remember him too," Meade said, eyeing Hogan with a combination of amusement and wariness.

Both Hedge and Meade noticed the change in Hogan. Three years ago he had been new to the owlhoot trail, but during that time he seemed to have grown much more sure of himself. Meade made the same observation about Hogan that Hogan had made about him: He had grown harder. Both men also remembered that Hogan had not been treated all that well the last time he was in Inferno.

"Well, Hogan," Hedge said, "what have you got for us?"

"Ten percent, right? That still the going rate?"

"That's it."

Hogan had already counted out a number of bills and banded them together. Now he took the bundle out of his saddlebag and tossed it on the desk. It landed with an impressive thump and both the mayor and the sheriff stared at it in surprise and disbelief.

"How much is there?" Hedge asked.

"Two thousand five hundred."

"Well," Hedge said, "you seem to have done all right for yourself."

"I didn't do too bad."

"Just the two of you?"

"There's more coming," Hogan said, deliberately neglecting to mention how many.

Hedge studied the money on the desk for a few moments and then looked up at Hogan and his sidekick. "There is the small matter of a posse on your trail," the mayor said. "We might have to charge you a little extra for the added risk, Hogan."

"No risk," Hogan said. "We won't be staying long enough to put your town in danger."

That surprised both Hedge and Meade—and, for that matter, Daniels, and it wasn't his first surprise since they had entered the room. He had almost choked when Hogan threw twenty-five hundred dollars on the table. He wanted to know why Hogan had tossed Inferno twenty-five percent of their job instead of the required ten.

"You don't want to stay here in Inferno until the heat blows over?" Hedge asked.

"No. Just a day or two to rest up, and then we'll be on our way."

Hedge and Merade both became suspicious then. What did Hogan have in mind? Why would a man pay that much money just to stay in town two days at the most? It didn't make sense.

"Well, Hogan, you know the rules of the town. I'm sure you'll let your friend know."

"No cheating, no stealing and no killing," Hogan recited.

"Very good," Hedge said. "I'm happy that you still remember. All right, you might as well get yourselves settled in the hotel. We'll talk again, I'm sure."

Count on it, Hogan thought as he left the office, *only next time I'll do the talking*.

"Are you crazy?" Daniels demanded. They had taken

separate rooms at the hotel, but Daniels hadn't wasted any time knocking on Hogan's door.

"Why?"

"You know we made ten thousand on that bank job. Why the hell did you give that fat politician twenty-five hundred? That's one fourth, not ten percent."

"What are you worried about?" Hogan said. "It's my fourth, not yours."

"It better be."

"Besides," Hogan said, thinking about the spread he and Johnny could start with their share of the money, "I'll be getting it back."

"You knew those men, didn't you?"

"I already told you, Matt. I've been here before. Sure, I know them, and they think they know me, but right now they're not so sure they do."

"What's he got in mind?" Meade asked Hedge after Hogan and Daniels had left the office.

"I don't know," Hedge said. "He's changed. He wasn't that sure of himself three years ago."

"He wasn't nothing three years ago."

"Well, he's changed, and I don't like it." Hedge picked up the money that was on the desk and said, "And he's still got over twenty thousand dollars."

"That I like," Meade said with a greedy grin.

"Yes," Hedge said, "I have to agree with you there, Meade. There is definitely something about that that I like very much too."

The next morning Clint and Demi dressed in their room in strained silence, but while they were buckling on their gun-belts she tried one more time to talk him out of his crazy idea.

"Demi, we went over this all last night. It's the only way. I hope you're going to do your part for me."

"Of course I am," she said, annoyed that he would even question her about it. "If I can't talk you out of it you know I'm going to help you."

"Then you'd better get going. I'll meet you at the livery stable."

"All right."

She left the hotel and went directly to the telegraph office and sent the message that Clint had instructed her to send. He told her to wait for the reply, and it came fairly quickly in the form of a bank draft from a man named Buckskin Frank Leslie. Clint told her that he had a piece of a saloon that Frank Leslie owned, and all she had to do was wire asking for the money and he would send it without question.*

Once she had the draft she was to go to the bank and cash it, and then meet Clint at the livery. Hopefully, the incident wouldn't get back to the bartender—or whoever was doing the spotting for Inferno—but even if it did, all they had was a woman withdrawing some money from the bank.

When Demi got to the livery, Clint was in the process of stealing a horse.

"You can't get away with this," the liveryman was saying while Clint tied him up, blindfolded him and then gagged him, cutting off his protestations.

Clint saddled the horse—with a stolen saddle, of course—and walked it to the front entrance of the livery, where he met Demi.

"Did you get it?"

"I did," she said. "Frank Leslie must be a special friend of yours to hand over a thousand dollars to a woman he doesn't even know."

"He is," Clint assured her, taking the money.

"Time to go, huh?"

"Time to go, yeah," he said, tucking the money away. "Give me a half hour and then untie the liveryman. He's bound to sound the alarm. After that you can tell the sheriff that I stole your money after a night of illicit pleasures—as long as you can do it without getting too embarrassed."

"The thing I'm going to have to do is keep from laughing," she said, shaking her head. "You're a crazy man, Clint Adams, but you better come back to me in one piece."

"Don't worry, I intend to."

*The Gunsmith #16: Buckskins and Six-guns

Hastily she threw her arms around his neck, kissed him soundly and said, "Good luck."

He patted her fanny, mounted up and rode out of town, heading in the direction they had last tracked their prey. Clint hoped he wouldn't have to ride around aimlessly for too long before he found Inferno. He knew one thing, though.

He *was* going to find it!

Chapter Eighteen

It was a weary and bedraggled—but excited—Clint Adams who rode down the main street of what he felt sure was the town of Inferno. It looked like any other town, with its general store and a hardware store—even a *bank*, for Christ's sake—but Clint knew that the difference between this and any other town was that the men who ran those establishments had prices on their heads.

This is it, he told himself, and the only thing that kept it from being perfect was not having Duke beneath him. He and his big buddy had been through a lot together, and he would have liked to share this feeling with him.

He considered whether he should be feeling more doubt and trepidation, but when he thought it over, why should he? He wasn't a lawman anymore. There was really no reason for anyone to sound an alarm if they happened to recognize him. The only men who had anything to fear from him were the ones who had robbed the bank in Phoenix and killed two people, and he and those men had one thing in common: He didn't know what they looked like, and they didn't know him either—or the fact that he was part of the posse that was after them.

Riding down the main street, he was aware that he was attracting a certain amount of attention, but he was determined to act if he were simply entering any other town. He rode to the livery where he put up his horse and ignored the stares of the liveryman, and then he went to the hotel to register. He recognized many of the names that had registered before him, although he did not see anyone listed whom he knew personally. He signed his own name. Accepted the key from the clerk, ignoring the looks *he* was giving him, and took his gear upstairs to his room.

Now he had a decision to make. The powers that be in Inferno would certainly be informed that he was in town. Should he simply wait in his room for them, or continue to do what he would normally do when he arrived in a town? Actually, it was his thirst that decided for him, and he left the hotel and walked to the nearest saloon.

When he entered the crowded saloon, conversation died down and everyone watched him as he walked to the bar.

"Beer," he told the bartender, whom he immediately recognized from an old flyer. He was Bad Bryon Brown, who had disappeared from sight some ten years before with a price of two hundred dollars on his head. He'd put on some weight, presumably from his sedentary life of tending bar, but he was still recognizable.

Brown brought the beer over and set it down on the bar in front of him. "Just get into town?"

"That's right."

"Plan on staying long?"

"What if I am?" Clint asked, trying to sound put upon by the question.

"Don't get yourself in an uproar, mister," Brown said, "I was just asking."

"Well, don't," Clint snapped back. "If I should get the urge to confide in somebody, I'll let you know."

Brown frowned and looked around at some of the other men in the room, but *he* was a part of Inferno, and the other men in the saloon were just staying there. It was up to him to find out something that he could pass on to Meade and Hedge.

"Mister, do you know what town you're in?"

"Now that's a good question," Clint said, putting his beer

back down on the bar. "I didn't see any signposts outside of town, and there are none on any of the stores, so I guess I don't rightly know what town I'm in. You care to tell me?"

Brown was unsure of what to do. He didn't recognize the man himself, and no one in the room had given any indication of recognizing him. Should he back off and wait until Harry at the hotel gave the man's name to Meade?

"I reckon you'll find that out soon enough," Brown said, wiping the bar top with a rag.

Clint knew that he could have played it harder, but why step too far out of character and make it obvious?

"Doesn't matter, anyway," he muttered, "as long as the beer's cold and there's some loose women around."

He looked around the room, examining it by the reflection in the mirror behind the bar, and there were some women scattered about. It had taken him the better part of the day—and a huge amount of luck—to stumble into Inferno, so it was late, and the saloon was full.

Now that they'd had their look at him the conversation gradually began to build up again, although in some cases he was sure that he was the topic of discussion. In the corner a piano player started up, and pretty soon the sound was deafening and very few people were paying attention to him.

Still using the mirror he looked around the room, recognizing a face here and there from old wanted posters. He saw a couple of people—Jimmy Stark and Cool Hannibal Carter—whom he had thought dead, and others—like Jack Foxx—who had simply dropped out of sight.

Some of them, he was sure, were simply there lying low for a while, while others were in retirement. He wondered what the arrangements were. Were they allowed to stay as long as they wanted, for nothing, or were they paying some kind of a fee?

Finishing his beer he decided to go back to the hotel. Having recognized some of the faces, he was now convinced that he was indeed in the legendary outlaw town of Inferno. Now his problem was identifying the men he had come here to catch, and getting out alive with them.

* * *

"There's a stranger in town," Meade told Hedge.

"Oh? Who is he?"

"He signed at the hotel as Clint Adams," Meade said, watching Hedge's face. "That name mean anything to you?"

"Sure," Hedge said, putting his pen down and staring at his sheriff. "The Gunsmith."

"Right. What are we going to do?"

"We'll treat him like anyone else," Hedge answered. "Bring him to me and I'll tell him the rules. If he doesn't like it, he can leave."

"Wait a minute, I don't think you understand this. This is the Gunsmith we're talking about. The man used to be a lawman. He wore a badge for years."

"And if I remember correctly he hasn't worn a badge for some years now."

"So?"

"So check him out. What direction did he ride in from?"

"North."

"Check with our people in Driftwood and see what his story is. If he's here to cool off, fine, but if he's here for some other reason . . ."

"Like to shut us down?"

Nodding, Hedge said, "Then the legend of the Gunsmith will come to an end right here in Inferno. What could be more fitting?"

Chapter Nineteen

When the knock on Clint's door came he was not surprised, although he was not expecting it quite so soon. The man standing there when he opened the door was big and rough-hewn, in his late thirties, wearing a battered silver star on his chest.

"Are you Clint Adams?" he asked gruffly.

"That's right."

"Come with me."

"Is that a request or an order?"

The man frowned and said, "The mayor of the town would like to see you."

"I guess that's as close to a request as I'm going to get," Clint said, picking up his hat. "Lead the way, Sheriff—?"

"Meade."

As Clint followed the sheriff to the town hall he thought about the name Meade. He had known someone by that name once, but it wasn't this man. He hadn't been keeping up with the wanted posters over the past three or four years, but he was fairly sure there would be one on the sheriff, and probably on the mayor too.

At the town hall Meade led him down a hallway and through a door into a small office. The man seated behind the desk was carrying too much weight, and didn't bother trying to lift it out of his chair. He looked to be in his early fifties and was apparently going to seed in a hurry.

"Thank you, Sheriff, for bringing our new guest to see me." The mayor looked at Clint then and said, "Mr. Adams, my name is Hedge. I'm the mayor of this town."

"This town," Clint repeated. "That's what the sheriff said. Why does everyone have such an aversion to telling me the name of 'this town?' "

"You're curious about that, are you?"

"Only because it seems to be such an all-fired secret."

"Well, I'll be glad to tell you the name of our town, and then maybe you'll understand."

"Fine."

"Our town is called Inferno, Mr. Adams. Does that mean anything to you?"

"Well, I've heard of Inferno—but no, that's just a myth, an old wives' tale."

Hedge shook his head slowly and said, "I'm afraid it's not, Mr. Adams. *This is* Inferno."

Clint remained silent so that they would think that he was letting the information settle in.

"You used to be a lawman, Mr. Adams," Hedge went on. "What's that mean to you?"

"That was a long time ago."

"And what does being here in Inferno mean to you?"

"It's just another town."

"Just another town," Hedge repeated. "That's quite an attitude to take."

"What kind of attitude would you like me to take? Awe? Shock? Disbelief?"

Hedge thought a moment and then said, "I suppose any one of those might be appropriate."

"Sorry I can't oblige you. I'm beyond being shocked or awed, and if you want to name your town Inferno, who am I to disbelieve you?"

"I see," Hedge said then. "You still don't believe that this is *the* Inferno of the legend."

"If you say it is, then it is."

"I'm afraid we also have some rules here, Mr. Adams, that even the famous Gunsmith will have to abide by."

"What kind of rules?"

"We run a nice, quiet, peaceful town. There is to be no stealing, no cheating and no killing."

"That's sounds reasonable."

"In addition there is a fee for being allowed to stay in our town."

"If I remember by legend correctly it's ten percent, isn't it?"

"It is. Ten percent of the amount of your last job? Have you pulled a bank holdup, or a stage holdup of late?"

Meade smirked at that question, because he had checked up on Adams and found out what his "last job" was.

"You probably already know the answer to that," Clint said.

Hedge looked at Meade and said, "Do we, Meade?"

"We do. The word from Driftwood is that he and a lady checked into the hotel together and the next morning Adams stole a horse and made off with the lady's money."

Hedge gave Clint a disappointed look and said, "Hardly conduct becoming a man of your reputation."

"You can't eat or ride a reputation."

"So true. How much did Mr. Adams take from the lady, Sheriff?"

"She says a thousand dollars."

"Is that true?" Hedge asked Clint.

"I could lie, but why start out on the wrong foot? Yeah, it's true."

"In that case, your fee is one hundred dollars, payable now."

Clint took a roll of bills from his pocket and counted out one hundred dollars. He dropped it on the desk and put the rest of it away.

"That cover it?"

"Of course you'll have to pay your hotel bill, and pay for your meals—"

"Just like in any other town."

"Yes, except for one thing. Here in Inferno we also require a fee of twenty-five dollars to be paid each week. That is nonnegotiable. If you do not pay it, or if you fall behind, you will be asked to leave by the sheriff and his deputies."

Clint studied Hedge in silence for a few moments, then took out the bills and counted off twenty-five more dollars.

"First week in advance," he said, dropping it on the desk.

"I like your style, Mr. Adams, and I must say that I'm sorry to see that you have fallen on somewhat hard times. Hopefully, better times are coming."

"Hopefully. It is all right if I go back to my room now? I'm kind of tired."

"Please, feel free. Our town is your town. We have some excellent saloons and some excellent women. If you go down the street to Georgia's I'm sure you will find something you like to warm your bed."

"That's okay," Clint said. "I'm not hard up enough to pay for a woman."

Clint turned to leave, but Hedge wasn't through yet. "There's one more little thing."

"What's that?"

"There might be one or two people here who might remember you from your lawman days. If they do, and they should take exception to your presence, I hope you will be able to find some other means of solving it than with your gun. The rules, you know."

"As long as they play by the rules, I will too."

"I warn you, whichever man is left standing after a gun battle will be severely reprimanded."

"That's a comforting thought," Clint said. "I'm sure that will go through everyone's mind right off."

"I am just asking you to remember my warning."

"Don't worry," the Gunsmith said, "I have a great memory."

Chapter Twenty

"New man in town, huh?" a voice said from Clint's right as he leaned on the bar.

After leaving Hedge's office he had gone straight to the saloon and ordered another beer. This time his appearance did not elicit quite the response it had before, but he still felt that he was the object of much attention. No one had approached him, though, until now.

The voice was distinctly female, though smoky, and when he turned his head to see who it was he was pleasantly surprised. She was no kid, but then Clint's preference of late had been running to the experienced type.

This one had dark black hair piled on her head, big brown eyes, and a ready smile on her ripe mouth. He got an immediate impression of brashness and intelligence.

"I guess I'm the newest man in town, so you must be talking to me, right?"

"Buy a lady a drink?"

"Sure."

She was small, not over five-two or so, and she had a compact, full-breasted body that she pressed against him now.

"You wouldn't be lonely, would you, mister?"

"All the time," he said, as the bartender brought him a beer, "but not if it will cost me more than this beer."

She looked at him speculatively and said, "You don't like to pay for your pleasures, huh?"

"I'll pay for a good drink or a good meal with no problem, but a good woman is an entirely different matter."

She picked up her beer and touched her lips to it, so that they were covered with foam, then licked it off enticingly.

"Well," she said, "I get paid the same amount of money whether I get any from you or not, and I have to say that when you came in I . . . felt something. If you've a mind not to be lonely tonight, I'm more than willing . . ."

He looked at her and said, "My hotel room?"

She shook her head. "I have a room upstairs. It's clean, and it's mine. Won't nobody bother us there."

"All right," he said, taking a last sip from his beer and setting the mug down on the bar, "lead the way."

As he followed her swaying hips up the steps it occurred to him, of course, that someone could have put her up to it, but as long as he was aware of that possibility there was no immediate threat. If she was for real, then there was also the possibility that he could get some information from her that might lead him to the men he wanted.

When she let them into her room with a key, he found that she hadn't been lying. The room was neat and clean, not the kind of room you'd expect a saloon girl to take a man up to.

"I told you," she said, reading the look in his eyes, "this is my room. I don't bring just anybody up here."

"I'm flattered."

She closed the door and locked it behind them. "What's your name?"

"Clint. What's yours?"

"Suzanne. Kiss me."

He gathered her in, enjoying the solid feel of her in his arms, and kissed her. She nibbled at his bottom lip, then sent her tongue on an exploration trip into his mouth.

Sliding his hands up her back he found the catch at the back of her dress and undid it, then helped her out of it. She broke the kiss long enough to discard her underthings and shoes, then threw herself at him again, kissing him while she helped him with his clothes.

When he was naked she dropped to her knees, and he cradled her head in his hands while she took him into her mouth and sucked him avidly. When she felt him swelling and his legs begin to tremble she released him and dropped down onto the bed. He examined her full dark brown-nippled breasts, her chunky thighs and hips and the dark tangle of hair between her legs, and then set about to enjoy what he was seeing.

"We aren't going to be interrupted, are we?" he asked her at one point.

"God, no," she said, her hips twitching anxiously. "You thinkin' maybe somebody set me on you?"

"I'm thinking it's a possibility," he said, "and I'd sure hate to be interrupted now."

"So would I, Clint, so would I. Don't worry, we're all alone and will be for as long as we like."

He lowered his head and probed the tangle of hair between her legs with his tongue until he found her moist nest, and then began to lick eagerly. Sliding his hands beneath her he cupped her firm buttocks and lifted her off the bed while he licked and sucked at her, making her catch her breath and gather up handfuls of sheets. When he felt her belly begin to tremble he knew she was about to explode and fastened his lips onto her clit and sucked furiously.

"Oh, God, yes!" she cried, beating her fists against the bed, thrusting her crotch up into his face. "Yes, suck me, suck me hard, that's it . . ."

After giving her one last long, loving lick, he crawled on top of her. She took him by the buttocks and hurriedly drew him inside of her and then began to buck like a filly who's never felt the saddle before.

"Oh, yes," she said afterward, "I was right about you, wasn't I?"

"How's that?"

"I just knew you'd come alive in my bed," she said. "I could tell by looking at you. You look so calm and sure of yourself, and I knew when I got you in my bed what it would be like."

"You're an exciting woman, Suzanne," he told her. "You'd make any man perform beyond himself."

"Not you," she said, shaking her head and regarding him with those big moist brown eyes. "I think you just naturally do the best you can all the time."

"I try."

"What brings you to Inferno, Clint?"

"Actually, I didn't know it was Inferno when I got here, and to tell the truth I still don't know that it's *that* Inferno."

"If there's another one, the country is in trouble," she said seriously. "This is it, all right, Clint. All you have to do is recognize some of those men downstairs to know that."

"Like who?"

"Like Jack Foxx, like Denver John Doyle, like the bartender, Bad Byron Brown—"

"That was Bryon Brown?" he asked, acting surprised.

"That's him."

"He dropped out of sight years ago with a price on his head."

"He came here and stayed, like a lot of the others did."

"And he's been paying twenty-five dollars a week since then?"

She looked uncomfortable now, as if she suddenly realized that she had been talking too much. "You won't tell anyone we talked about this, will you?"

"Of course not, Suzanne."

"Well, there are certain people that don't have to pay the twenty-five a month. Hedge's people, and Byron is one of them."

"Like Meade?"

"Meade's the sheriff. He collects, he don't pay."

"What about you?" he asked. "What brought you here?"

She looked up at the ceiling and said, "I came with a man I thought I loved, and I ended up working in the saloon."

"Who was the man?"

She looked at him, grinned ironically and said, "Meade."

Chapter Twenty-One

Clint left Suzanne in her room—"To repair the damages," she said—and went downstairs. Meade was standing at the bar, talking to Brown.

Clint had been able to keep Suzanne talking for a while and she had finally told him that a couple of strangers had arrived in town the day before. She didn't know who they were, although she was sure that Meade and Hedge did. She didn't know which of the two hotels they were staying at.

As Clint reached the foot of the steps Meade turned in response to something Brown had said and looked directly at Clint. He waved Clint over, and the Gunsmith walked to the bar.

"Buy you a drink?"

"I was about to turn in."

Meade looked up the steps toward Suzanne's room and said, "She's something, isn't she?"

"If you're talking about Suzanne, I'd have to agree."

"How about that drink?"

"Sure, I can stand one more. I'll take a beer."

"Byron, give the man a beer."

"Sure, Meade."

"Yours is kind of an unusual situation, Adams," Meade said to him when he had his beer.

"How's that?"

"Well, I don't think we've ever had an ex-lawman in town

before." Meade spoke in a normal tone, apparently uncon-
cerned about being overheard.

"I guess I should feel honored."

"Unless you're not an *ex*-lawman," Meade added, eyeing
Clint suspiciously. "If that was the case, you'd be in a lot of
trouble, wouldn't you."

"Maybe."

Meade waited and when Clint didn't say anything further
the sheriff said, "Well, are you?"

"Meade," Clint said, putting his beer down on the bar
virtually untouched, "right now you're more of a lawman
than I am. How long have you worn that badge?"

"Five years."

"Sort of makes you wonder, don't it?" Clint asked.
"Have a nice night."

Clint walked to the batwing doors without glancing around
and pushed through them. It was dark, and the main street of
Inferno was lit by streetlamps. Clint stepped onto the dirt and
started toward his hotel. Was Meade suspicious for any
reason other than a natural inclination? He hoped not. It was a
little too soon for him to have to worry about getting out of
Inferno alive.

Chapter Twenty-Two

In the morning Clint stopped by the front desk of the hotel and asked the clerk where the best place in town was to get a good breakfast. The man told him to go to Max's café. When Clint heard the first name he asked, "Max? What's his last name?"

"Price," the clerk said. "Max Price, mister."

"Max Price?"

"The same."

"He's running a café?"

"And doing all the cooking."

"Son of a bitch."

Clint left the hotel thinking, *I'll be goddamned. Max Price!* Price and Clint were contemporaries. They had come out west and found themselves in Oklahoma at the same time. From that point on their careers had taken very different paths, with Max traveling the owlhoot trail while Clint took up the badge. He hadn't heard anything of Price in over five years, and he hurriedly walked to the café, eager to see Max again.

When he entered the café he saw that the place was apparently very popular with the people of the town. A tired-looking waitress with listless blond hair told him that he'd have to wait for a table.

"That's okay," he said. "Is Max in the back?"

The girl really looked at him for the first time and asked, "You know Max?"

"We're old friends."

"He don't like to be bothered while he's cooking."

"That's tough," Clint said. He pointed to a doorway in the back of the room and asked, "Does that lead to the kitchen?"

"Yeah, but—"

"Excuse me."

"He stepped past her and strode boldly across the room to the kitchen, drawing the interest of everyone in the room. Bets started flying about, with odds as to how long it would take Max Price to send the stranger flying back through the doorway.

Max Price, looking as lean and tough as ever, stood in front of a stove wearing a white apron and a gunbelt over it with the gun worn low on his left hip. Clint remembered Max Price as a man who was ghost-fast with a gun.

"Price, you son of a bitch," he said aloud.

"What—" Price started to say, turning his head to see who was interrupting him. When he saw Clint Adams standing there his jaw dropped and he said, "Are you crazy?"

"Nice to see you too, Max."

"What the hell are you doing here?" Price demanded, bearing down on Clint. "Do you even know where you are? Are you trying to get yourself killed?"

"Whoa, slow down, and I'll answer one or two of those questions. What I'm doing here is looking for a good break-fast. Yes, I know where I am, and no, I'm not looking to get killed. You got any more questions?"

Price grabbed him by both arms and shook him, demand-ing, "How the hell are you?"

Clint took hold of Price's arms in return and said, "I'm fine, Max, and surprised to find you still alive. I'm not surprised to find you in the kitchen, though. You always did like to cook."

"Yeah," Price said sheepishly. "I guess I would have been most happy working some chuckwagon, but this ain't bad." Suddenly Price looked directly at Clint's chest, and the Gunsmith knew what he was looking for.

"No badge, Max, not for a long time, now."

"Got tired of it?"

"Yeah."

"I knew you would. But what the hell are you doing here?"

Clint shrugged and said, "Just wandered in without knowing where I was."

"You must have been pretty surprised to find out you were in Inferno, huh?"

"I was surprised, yeah, but not as surprised as I was to find you here. How long have you been here?"

" 'Bout five years, now, I guess. I—"

At that moment the waitress walked in looking puzzled, because she more than anyone else had expected Price to throw the stranger out on his butt. "Max, we got customers waiting," she said, studying both men curiously.

"Clint, I want you to meet my wife. Diane, this is my old friend, Clint Adams. You get him a table right quick. I'm gonna whip him up a breakfast like he ain't never had." Price looked at Clint and said, "Go with Diane, Clint. I got meals to get out, so we'll talk later. Okay?"

"Sure, Max, sure."

Clint turned and followed the woman outside, and she led him to a table.

"Max is always talking about you," she told him. "I never thought I'd get to meet you, though."

"I never thought I'd get to see Max again."

She looked around at some of the other impatient diners and said to Clint, "I got to handle these people, Clint. Can I get you some coffee?"

"Strong and black."

She smiled, which made her seem less listless and tired, and said, "That's the only kind we got."

Max Price, he thought, watching Mrs. Price calm down some of the impatient customers. It was just as much of a surprise to find him married. Max had always been a ladies' man, and Clint was a little surprised at his choice of wives. Not that Diane Price wasn't attractive, but Max had always leaned toward the more flashy type.

When the breakfast came it was as Max had said, like none the Gunsmith had ever had before. There were scrambled eggs, potatoes, ham *and* steak, homemade biscuits, jam and butter, and more coffee.

"More coffee?" Diane Price asked.

"No, ma'am. Two pots is enough."

"How was it?"

"Just like Max said it would be. You tell him I said so, okay? I don't want to go back there and bother him again."

"You could," she assured him. "You're the only person other than me he's ever allowed back there."

"I'm honored. It was a pleasure meeting you, Diane. What do I owe you for breakfast?"

"Nothing," she said, shrugging. "Max insisted."

"Tell Max I'll be by later. We've got a lot of catching up to do."

"He'll be looking forward to it," she said, and then added, "And so will I."

Clint left the café, feeling a certain elation at having found a lost friend that almost made him forget why he was there in Inferno. Seeing Suzanne walking toward him, obviously heading for breakfast, brought it back to him.

She was walking with her head down and didn't see him until she was almost up to him. When she raised her head the surprise showed on her face, and she turned quickly to walk away.

"Suzanne, wait!" he called, but instead of stopping she quickened her pace. He hurried to catch up to her and put his hand on her shoulder to turn her around. When he did he saw the swollen and bruised area around her right eye.

"What happened?"

"Nothing. Let me go."

"Who did that to you?" he demanded.

"No one," she insisted, but it suddenly came to him who it had to be.

"Meade? Did Meade do that to you, Suzanne?"

She hesitated a moment and then nodded nervously. "If he sees me talking to you—"

"Don't worry about it," he told her. "You were going to have breakfast, weren't you?"

"Y-yes."

"Well, go ahead. I won't bother you. At least, not until I've had a talk with Meade."

"Clint—"

"Go on, and don't worry."

He gave her a little shove in the direction of the café, and then headed for Meade's office.

He entered without knocking, and Meade, seated at his desk with a cup of coffee, looked up. A younger man, wearing a deputy's badge, was there too.

"Get lost," Clint said to the deputy.

"What?" the man asked in disbelief. He looked at the sheriff with an amused expression, but Meade simply nodded.

"Go on, Will. I'll see you later."

"But he can't—"

"Maybe not, but I can," Meade interrupted him. "Go on." When the deputy grudgingly left the office Meade said to Clint, "What's on your mind?"

"Suzanne."

"What about her?"

"I don't have any respect for a man who'd slap a woman around, Meade, which I guess means that I have even less respect for you than I did yesterday."

Meade's eyes narrowed dangerously and he stood up.

"You make a move for that gun, Meade, and I'll kill you where you stand. Who'll reprimand me if that happens?"

Meade wanted to draw, but the Gunsmith's reputation kept him from doing so. There was only one man in town that Meade thought might be able to match the Gunsmith with a gun. There were three or four who would *think* that they could, but only one who'd have a chance.

Max Price.

"Have your say, Adams."

"If you touch that woman one more time, for any reason, I'll come back and I will kill you, Meade. Don't have any doubt about that."

"You're talking to the law in Inferno, Adams," Meade reminded him.

"That's right," Clint said, *"you're* the law, Meade, not

me, so don't be beating up on a woman because of what you think she might tell me. *You're* the lawman, so you're the one who doesn't belong here.''

From Meade's stunned silence Clint knew that he'd started the man thinking. The whole point of Inferno was that a man could come here to get away from the law.

What did that make Meade?

Chapter Twenty-Three

Clint knew that his conversation with Meade would bring some kind of response. What he didn't know was the form it would take.

He might have been surprised if he did.

"Come on in, Max," Mayor Mike Hedge said. Price had gotten word that Hedge wanted to see him, and when the crowd at the café thinned out to a point where Diane could handle it, he walked over to the town hall to see what it was all about.

"What's on your mind, Mike?" he asked, taking a seat. He had discarded the apron, but the forty-five was ever-present on his left hip.

"We have a potential problem, Max, which you might be able to help us with."

"I'll do what I can."

"I told Meade you'd help."

"Meade?" Price asked, his distaste for the sheriff showing on his face.

"Let's not dredge up old news, Max. Let me tell you what the problem is."

"I wish you would. I left Diane alone at the café."

"How is Diane?"

"She's fine, Mike. Could we get to the point, please?"

"Sure, Max, sure." Mike Hedge tiptoed quite a bit when

he was in Max Price's presence. Price was possibly the only man in Inferno who couldn't be controlled completely—with the possible exception now, of course, of Clyde Hogan. In addition, Price was the only man that Mike Hedge was . . . careful of.

He would never admit to being afraid of Price, but that was what it boiled down to.

"The problem," Hedge said, "is Clint Adams, the Gunsmith."

"What about him?"

"I hear he went into your kitchen this morning and didn't get thrown out on his ear. That's kind of unusual, isn't it, Max?"

"Clint Adams is a friend."

"Ah, that explains it."

"What's the problem? He's not a lawman anymore."

"So he says."

"You got any reason to doubt him?"

"Not at the moment."

"But you're looking for one."

"I'm just being careful, Max. The welfare of Inferno and its citizens *is* my welfare, you know."

"Uh-huh. What is it you want from me, Mike?"

"Well, if the Gunsmith should prove a problem, Max, we would, uh, need someone who was . . . handy with a gun, just in case—"

"You want me to go up against the Gunsmith?"

"Well, if the need arose, you'd be the logical choice, wouldn't you?"

"Why?"

"You're the only man who would stand a chance of beating him, Max."

"No," Price said, "you've got plenty of gunhands in this town, Mike. Any one of them would be tickled to go up against the Gunsmith. I'm afraid I don't agree with you on this one. I'm a cook, not a gunman."

Hedge pointedly looked at the gun on Max Price's hip, and Price himself looked down at it.

"You know I can't take my gun off, Mike. I'd be a dead man if I did."

"I hope you'll reconsider, Max," Hedge said as Price stood up to leave. "If Adams becomes a problem, I'm afraid we'd be calling on you to help us. You're a citizen of Inferno, Max. You'd have to make a choice."

"When the time comes," Price said, "if there's a choice to make, I'll make it and stand by it, but I'll make it on my own, Hedge."

Price's eyes grew cold and bore into Mike Hedge's, and the mayor found himself looking away. As Price left, Hedge was thinking that he wouldn't mind all that much if it was the Gunsmith who came out on top in that confrontation.

He wouldn't mind at all.

Max Price walked back to his café, puzzling over the recent turn of events, most specifically the appearance of Clint Adams in Inferno—by accident? He had never known Clint Adams to do anything purely by accident. True, he hadn't seen his old friend in years, but people don't change that much, do they? Even he, who no longer made his way with his gun, hadn't changed all that much.

What was Clint doing in Inferno? He wasn't a lawman and Price knew damn well that the Gunsmith hadn't taken to the owlhoot trail. So why was he here, and what would Price do if his presence did start to present a threat to Inferno? Price had a life here, the kind of life he couldn't have elsewhere because he was still a wanted man.

Clint was coming by later to talk, but Price figured that maybe he ought to do more listening than talking.

Chapter Twenty-Four

When Clint got back to Max's café he found that much of the crowd had melted away, and when Diane Price saw him she smiled and came toward him.

"Doesn't look so busy now," he commented.

"Not until lunch, anyway. Max isn't here right now, but he should be back soon."

"Oh? Where'd he go?"

"Over to the town hall to talk to Mike Hedge. He's the mayor here, you know—but you must know that. You would have had to talk to him by now."

"We've talked, yes."

"Would you like to come in the back while I clean up?"

"Sure."

In the kitchen she offered him a cup of coffee, which he accepted, and they talked idly while she cleaned the stove.

"Max insists that the stove be cleaned after every shift. He says his food tastes better that way."

"I guess he should know," Clint said. "Tell me where you and Max met, Diane."

"Right here in Inferno. Met here and got married here."

"I know what must have brought Max here. What was it that brought you here?"

She was about to answer when Price walked in.

"Here's Max."

"You've got a customer outside, Diane," Price said. His

face looked troubled, and Clint had a hunch he knew what Hedge had wanted to see him about.

"I'll take care of him," she said, and hurried out of the kitchen.

Price and Clint stared at each other a few moments, and then Price said, "You making waves, Clint?"

"What do you mean?"

"We been friends too long to diddle each other," Price said, "even if it has been a while since we saw each other. Hedge wanted to know if I would be available if and when you got to be a problem."

"And?"

"And what? *Are* you going to be a problem?"

Clint didn't answer right away and Price walked to the stove and took up where his wife had left off.

"I'm waiting for an answer."

"I might be a problem, Max, yes," Clint finally said, deciding to be honest.

"Shit," Price said, leaning on the stove. "Why don't you ride out now, Clint, before that happens?"

"I can't, Max. I came here for something and I can't leave without it."

"I don't want to know what or who you came here for," Price said. "That ain't my business, but if you start to pose a threat to the town, Clint, that would become a problem."

"What did you tell Hedge, Max?"

"I told him that I'd make my decision if and when the time came." Price looked at Clint and said, "I hope it doesn't come to that, Clint."

"So do I, Max," Clint said with sincerity, "so do I."

There was an awkward silence, which Clint broke by saying, "I guess this isn't the moment to go over old times, Max."

"I guess it ain't."

"I'll see you later."

"Sure."

Clint left the café, saying a quick good-bye to a puzzled Diane Price. This was a complication Clint hadn't foreseen—to have an old friend pop up, and then face the possibility of having to fight him.

He decided that the only way to deal with it was Price's way. Make that decision when the time came.

He just hoped that it would never come.

Diane Price watched Clint Adams leave the café, then went back to the kitchen, wondering how two old friends could have gone over old times so quickly. Something was wrong.

"Max?"

"What's the order?"

She gave him the customer's order and then asked, "Why did Clint leave so soon?"

"He had to go."

"What's wrong, Max?"

"Nothing," Price said, breaking three eggs into a bowl.

"What did Mike want?"

"It's not important, Diane," Price said. "Check outside and see if there are any more customers, will you?"

She knew that when her husband got like this there was no way she could get anything out of him that he didn't want to give her. She also knew that when Price got like that, it meant trouble, and she was frightened.

Chapter Twenty-Five

When Clint got back to the hotel, the desk clerk was nowhere to be seen, so he took the opportunity to check through the register again and see who had signed in ahead of him. The name above his was Walt Sheldon, but he had registered a couple of weeks earlier. That meant that if the men he was looking for had come into town, they were staying at the other hotel.

He went up to his room to clean his guns, the modified forty-five, the New Line Colt and his Springfield rifle. Very soon now he might find himself needing them, and he wanted them operating at peak efficiency.

"What do you think?" Hedge asked Meade.

"I think I don't like being threatened by anyone!" Meade said stiffly.

"I'm not talking about that," Hedge said, shrugging the incident off. "That's what you get for hitting a woman."

"She's *my* woman!"

"She might have a different opinion about that—but that's not what we're here to talk about, Meade. I'm talking about Hogan's money, and Adams's presence in town."

"You want the money, don't you?"

"Damn right."

"So why should Adams's presence change things?"

"Because it's not easily explained," Hedge said, "and I

104

don't like things without explanations. Have Hogan's other men arrived yet?''

"No.''

"Then we've got some time, yet. Maybe the Gunsmith problem will resolve itself.''

"How?''

"Price. Maybe somebody should tell Price that they saw his wife visiting Adams in his room.''

"Price will kill him.''

Hedge smiled and said, "Exactly.''

"Well, what the hell is taking them so long to get here?'' Matt Daniels complained.

"Take it easy,'' Clyde Hogan told him. "Have another drink.''

Hogan started to call to the bartender, but Daniels said, "I don't want another drink, damn it, I want my money. You think that fool brother of yours got lost, or worse—caught?''

"Don't call him a fool,'' Hogan said tightly. He'll be here. Don't worry.''

"Yeah,'' Matt Daniels said.

"Go get yourself a woman, will you?''

"That's a good idea,'' Daniels said. "I'll see you later.''

"Sure.''

The truth was Clyde Hogan *was* worried about his brother. He should have been here by now, but maybe it was better this way. Maybe not having Johnny around when Hedge and Meade made their move was okay—and they would make a move, of that he was sure. He was counting on their collective greed to bring them to him, at which time he was going to kill them both, and then take back his money and leave Inferno and start that spread with Johnny.

Actually, he thought, getting a woman didn't sound like such a bad idea, especially if the woman was that dark-haired Suzanne.

Unaware that she was playing right into the hands of Hedge and Meade, Diane Price went to Clint Adams's hotel to see him.

When the knock sounded on his door, Clint couldn't imagine who it was. When he opened it, he was surprised to find Diane Price.

"Diane, hi."

"Can I come in for a moment, Clint?"

"Sure."

He stepped back and allowed the worried-looking woman to enter, then shut the door and turned to face her. He realized that if she weren't so tired looking she would be quite pretty. He doubted that she was as old as she looked, which was about thirty. She was probably closer to twenty-five.

"What's wrong?"

"That's what I wanted to ask you," she said. "What happened between you and Max?"

"Nothing. Why?"

"Don't tell me that. Max went to see Hedge, and then, when he came back, you and he talked for just a little while. Two old friends couldn't have possibly gone over old times so quickly. What happened? Please tell me."

"Diane, I wish I could, but if Max has a problem, he's got to tell you himself. I can't tell you for him."

"But you do know."

"I suspect that Hedge wants him to do something he doesn't want to do."

"And it has to do with you?"

"Possibly."

It struck Diane then what the similarities were between the Gunsmith and her husband. "You and Max, you both have reputations with a gun."

"Yes."

"Is that it? Does Hedge want Max to face you with a gun? But you're friends, you can't—"

"Diane, I have no intention of going against Max with a gun. You don't have to worry about that."

"I believe you," she said, "but that doesn't tell me what's the matter with Max."

"You're just going to have to wait for him to talk to you himself."

"I suppose so. I've got to get back. Thank you for talking to me."

"I wish I could have helped."

"You did," she said, opening the door, "now the rest is up to Max."

In Driftwood, Demi Templeton was becoming increasingly impatient. She had not heard from Clint and there had been no sign of John Russell or any of the other members of the posse. It was all she could do to keep from riding out and looking for Inferno on her own, but Clint's last argument had been his best and most irrefutable: He needed somebody on the outside just in case he got into trouble.

Now she was asking herself a question: How was she supposed to know when that was?

Chapter Twenty-Six

Clint decided against going to the café for lunch, and went to the saloon instead where he got involved in an early poker game. He didn't recognize the four other men in the game, and it didn't appear that any of them had recognized him. It helped that they did not bother to exchange names.

He was seated across from a fellow who looked to be about twenty-five or twenty-six. He had blond hair, and when he took his hat off to scratch his head, Clint noticed that it was remarkably flat. There was nothing particularly distinctive about the other three players, except that they were terrible at poker. The bulk of the winning was being done by the Gunsmith and the fellow with the flat head.

After about two hours of playing cards Clint looked up and saw Max Price bearing down on the table, glowering at him. There was no trace of friendship on Price's face.

"Hello, Max."

"I want to talk to you," Price said, "alone."

"Sure, Max," Clint said. "Deal me out, fellas." He gathered up his money and started to get up.

"You coming back?" the fella with the flat head asked.

"I don't know," Clint said. "Maybe."

Clint walked to an empty table with Price and they both sat down. "What's this all about, Max?"

"Did Diane come to your hotel room today?"

Frowning, Clint answered, "Yes, she did."

Price's face grew red and Clint was afraid that he knew what was happening.

"Why?" Price demanded.

"She wanted to talk to me."

"What about?"

"About you."

Price frowned. "You'd better explain."

"Have you asked her, Max?"

"I'm asking you."

"I don't like the way you're asking," Clint said. "I think you'd better talk to your wife."

"And I think you better stay away from her. I remember things about you, Clint. I remember that you liked women and they always seemed to like you."

"That's funny, I remember the same thing about you."

"Well, I'm married now, and even if I wasn't I'd never go after another man's wife."

"I think you better think about what you're saying, Max, before you go any further."

Price stood up and said, "Just remember what I'm telling you, Clint. Stay away from Diane."

"Max."

Price was turning to leave but he turned back to face Clint. "What?"

"Who told you that she came to my room?"

"That doesn't matter."

"I think it does," Clint said. "I think you should think about who it was that told you, and what they might have had to gain by it. Think about it, Max."

"Just remember what I said."

"I'll remember."

Price stalked out of the saloon. Clint was willing to bet that Price had heard about Diane's visit from Meade or one of his deputies. Hedge and Meade were playing it smart, trying to turn Price against Clint so that if and when the time came, he wouldn't hesitate to face him.

Clint just hoped that Max Price would be smart enough to see what they were doing before it was too late.

Chapter Twenty-Seven

That evening in the saloon Clint saw Suzanne. He thought for a moment that she was going to ignore him, but she walked over to stand by him at the bar and said, "Hi."

The swelling had gone down and the bruise circling her eye was barely noticeable.

"Looks fine."

She touched the area and said, "Powder. It does wonders for a girl."

"You don't need it."

She smiled. "Thanks, but I'm no kid, you know."

"I know," he said. "That's one of the things I like about you. Not afraid to be seen talking to me?"

"I don't know what you said to Meade, but it worked. He apologized for hitting me and told me not to worry about seeing you."

"That was nice of him. Did he ask you to report to him on anything we say together?"

She stared at him. "How did you know?"

"Just a hunch. Do as he says, Suzanne. I don't want you getting into trouble on my account."

"I can take care of myself. I was going to stay away from you so that you wouldn't get in trouble with Meade, but then he told me—"

"What? Who I was?"

She nodded and said, "The Gunsmith. Now I know that Meade won't want to tangle with you."

"Did he say that?"

"No, not him. He blustered on about how he wasn't afraid of you just because you had a reputation, but I could see it in his eyes. If he's not afraid of you, then he respects you. It amounts to the same thing."

When the bartender came with his beer, Clint ordered one for Diane.

"I saw you playing cards before with the other new arrival in town," she said.

"Other new arrival? Who are you talking about?"

"The one with the blond hair."

"And the square head?"

"That's the one. He only got into town the day before you did."

"Is that a fact?" Clint asked, trying to hide his eagerness. "What do you know about him?"

"Not much. He's come up to me a couple of times," she said, which was her way of saying that she'd slept with him. "His name is Clyde, and he's waiting for his brother and a friend to show up."

"Did he come alone?"

"No, he rode in with another man."

Waiting for his brother and a friend, and he rode in with another man. That made four, and the dead man they'd found on the trail was the fifth.

"And he's a stranger here?"

"Not really," she said. "He was here a few years ago, but I didn't get to know him then. Apparently he didn't have a happy visit."

"What makes you say that?"

"Just his attitude when he talks about it. He seems to think that the town owes him something."

"He's not staying at my hotel."

"No, he's at the other one." She stared at Clint for a moment and then asked, "Are you interested in him for some reason?"

"Not really. Besides, you're the one who brought him up, not me. I'm just trying to keep the conversation going."

She touched his arm and said, "I know a better place and a better way that we can do that."

Being with her again appealed to him all by itself, but the fact that she was suddenly supplying him with information made it even more appealing. "I'm all for that," he said, taking her arm. "Let's go."

After an energetic session in her bed Clint tried to gently pry some more information out of her, but there wasn't all that much that she knew. The newcomer's full name was Clyde Hogan and he called his brother Johnny; neither name rang a bell for Clint. She didn't know the names of the other two men.

When Clint came back downstairs he looked around the saloon, but there was no sign of Hogan. Should he march over to the man's hotel and confront him? He decided against that. Why not wait for the whole gang to be present? He had no way of singling out one man for the killings of the little girl and the deputy, so he was going to have to bring them all out singlehandedly, while avoiding conflicts with Max Price, Sheriff Meade or Mayor Hedge.

Looking around the saloon again he wondered if Clyde Hogan's partner was in the room. He was going to have to locate and identify that man as well, just so he'd know who he was up against.

He decided to go and take a look at Hogan's hotel and see if there was someplace he could hide and watch for Hogan and his partner. Hopefully they'd leave or return to the hotel together and he'd have them both identified.

At least he'd know who his enemies were—some of them anyway.

Chapter Twenty-Eight

"Do you know him?" Clyde Hogan asked.

Matt Daniels stared out the window at the man who had been standing across the street from the hotel for the better part of an hour. "No, I don't." Daniels turned and asked, "Why?"

"I played poker with him today, but we didn't exchange names. After I came back to the hotel I noticed him standing across the street. I didn't think anything of it until he was still there a half hour later. I checked the register and he's not registered here."

"How do you know that if you don't know his name?"

"Because nobody registered after us, and the last man to register before us was three weeks ago. No, he's registered at the other hotel, and I want to find out who he is."

"How?"

"We could go across the street and ask him."

"But you don't want to do that, do you?"

"No. I think maybe you ought to go over to his hotel and ask the desk clerk, instead."

"Why me?"

"Because he's seen me, and because you keep complaining that you're bored."

"I sure as hell am. All right, I'll check him out for you," Daniels said, walking to the door.

"For us, Matt," Clyde said correcting him. "If he's interested in me he might be interested in you too."

Daniels stopped short of the door and eyed Clyde Hogan speculatively. "You think he's part of the posse?"

Hogan considered that a moment and said, "If he was, would he be fool enough to come into this town by himself?"

"I guess that would depend on who he was, wouldn't it?"

"And that's what you were on your way to find out. Use the back door so he doesn't see you."

"Right."

When Daniels left Hogan walked back to the window, stood to the side and peered across the street.

The man was gone.

Clint had changed his plan when he found that there was really no way to watch the hotel without being seen. He decided that he would watch the hotel anyway and *wait* to be seen. Maybe he could force Hogan and his friend into some sort of action that would work for him.

He was watching the windows that faced the street, and at one window in particular there was a little activity. From time to time the curtain would move, as if someone were trying to peer out without being seen.

At one point a man boldly pushed aside the curtain and looked out, and that was the giveaway. He couldn't see the man well enough to identify him, but he did see him clearly enough to know that he wasn't Clyde Hogan. He also knew that if either man was going to leave the hotel now, it wouldn't be by the front door.

When Matt Daniels left his hotel by the back door he was totally unaware that Clint Adams was watching him. The Gunsmith trailed Daniels to the other hotel, where Daniels engaged the clerk in conversation, during which he first threatened him and then finally paid for the information.

What information could Hogan and his friend possibly want from the clerk at his hotel? Well, he knew it wasn't his hat size. Now that the men knew who he was, what would they do? Run for it or make a move against him?

Only time would tell, but at least he knew them both by sight now.

"He must have followed you," Hogan said when Matt Daniels returned to his room.

"Why do you say that?"

"Because as soon as you left he was gone."

"Jesus Christ," Daniels said, "you mean he could have taken me out any time?"

"I take it you got a name?"

"Did I ever! Does the name Clint Adams mean anything to you?"

"Adams," Hogan said to himself. "Yeah, I think—"

"There's no think about it, Clyde. That man out there was the Gunsmith, and if he's after us we're as good as got."

"Don't tell me you're afraid of him," Clyde said, looking at the usually confident Daniels in surprise.

"I ain't afraid of many men, Clyde, but the Gunsmith sure as hell is on my list—and probably number one."

Daniels was sweating. Clyde could see that he was indeed afraid of the Gunsmith. Hogan himself, at twenty-six, was still too young and brash to realize that he too should have been afraid.

"I want my money, Clyde," Daniels said. "I want to get out of here."

"Look, nobody says he's after us."

"Then why was he out in front of our hotel? And why did he follow me?" Daniels strode toward the window and peered out. "And why is he down there again?"

"Maybe we'll find out," Clyde said calmly, "but I've got other things to do first."

"So what are we gonna do?"

"I think we'll do what he's doing," Clyde Hogan said with confidence. "We'll just wait."

When Clint thought—or hoped—that he had them nervous enough he gave into his stomach's hungry grumblings. Still determined to avoid Max's café he went looking for somewhere else to eat and decided on the hotel dining room.

Over dinner he started to form the opinion that there were a lot of things going on in Inferno, not the least of which were his efforts to capture Clyde Hogan and the rest of his gang. From what Suzanne had told him of her conversations with Clyde—and who was she relating *their* conversations to?—it seemed as if Clyde had some sort of grudge against Inferno, which would mean Meade and Hedge. He probably had something planned, and that could work in Clint's favor by keeping Hogan's mind otherwise occupied.

Then there was the problem with Max Price. Latching onto a woman—or vice versa—often changed a man, usually into some sort of a jealous animal. This seemed to be the case with Price, and Meade and Hedge had banked on that emotion. Clint, however, didn't need the extra added problem of Price's jealousy and was determined to steer entirely clear not only of Diane Price but of Max himself.

When Clint returned to his hotel room he found company waiting for him.

"Who let you in here?"

Suzanne smiled at him from his bed and said, "The desk clerk. He knows me."

Clint wondered if she was speaking in the Biblical sense.

"You have something in mind?" he asked.

"Well, I thought maybe we'd try your bed out, for a change."

"Yes," he said, taking off his gunbelt and hanging it on the bedpost, "that is a thought."

Chapter Twenty-Nine

Suzanne reached eagerly for Clint, impatient for him to undress and join her on the bed. As he put a knee on the bed, she took hold of his cock with both hands. He paused in that postion while she reached down and laved the swollen head with her tongue, wetting it and playing with it. She allowed it to enter her mouth and sucked just on the head while her hands stroked the long shaft. Soon it was pulsing in her hand, begging for release, and she denied it by wrapping one hand tightly around the base.

"Jesus, Suzanne . . ."

"Shhh," she said, tugging on him so that he would lie down next to her, "we have all night."

"We do?"

"I'm not working tonight," she whispered in his ear. "I'm playing."

"You seem pretty damn serious to me," he said, as she tightened her hold.

"I take my playtime very seriously."

She shimmied down so that she was kneeling between his legs and once again took him in her mouth. This time, however, she took much more than just the head, accommodating almost all of him, while she cupped his sac gently in one hand. She sucked on him avidly, her head bobbing up and down at an ever-increasing speed, moaning with the effort and pleasure of it. When she felt his juices building in his balls she laughed delightedly, and suddenly he was filling her mouth and she was taking it all in. His hips were bouncing on the bed and she moved her hands beneath him to cup his buttocks, still sucking him until he was completely dry.

"Now me," she said, lying down next to him. He was only too happy to oblige.

He got down between her legs and started probing her until his tongue slipped inside of her. He ran his tongue along her wet slit, tasting her juices, only occasionally coming into contact with her rigid clit. When he thrust his tongue inside of her as far as it would go, she gasped and raised her hips, and his nose prodded that tiny little nubbin, sending waves of pleasure jolting through her. Repaying the favor he slid his hands beneath her to cup her buttocks and then began to run his tongue around her love button at increasing speed. She was gasping aloud by the time her first orgasm came, and she let out a high, keening wail as her body was wracked by waves of pleasure—but he was not finished with her.

He began to lick her again, giving her time to recover, and then concentrated his efforts on the center of her sex again. This time he slid his hands out from beneath her and used his elbows to pin her thighs to the bed. She sensed what he was going to do and said, "Oh no, please . . . I have to be able to move . . ."

She stopped as he began to suck on her clit, and suddenly she was bucking and heaving on the bed, trying unsuccessfully to fight her way out from beneath the pressure of his elbows. Her pinioned thighs were trembling, as was her belly, and then she opened her mouth wide as if to scream.

"Christ!" she said, letting the word out in a long sigh. "Damn you, that was so good it was too good. Why'd you pin me down like that?"

"Why'd you tease *me*?" he returned, lying next to her.

"It was fun."

"Yes," he said, "it was."

"Clint?"

"Hmm?"

"Why are you here?"

He had been feeling a comfortable drowsiness following

their lovemaking, but her question acted like a bucket of cold water, waking him completely.

"Why?" he asked, and she heard the suspicion in his tone.

"Oh, no, don't think I'm asking for—for Meade," she said hurriedly. "No, I was wondering . . . for myself, when you would be . . . leaving."

"When I've finished what I came here to do."

"I see."

"Why?"

"I . . . was just wondering . . ."

"What, Suzanne?"

She turned her head on the pillow and looked at him. "I was wondering if you might have—if you might be able to—to take me out with you."

"You want to leave Inferno?"

"God, yes!"

"Why haven't you left before now?"

"Meade," she said, making a face. "He won't let me leave."

"You've tried?"

"Yes. He says only those with a price on their head can leave, because they need the town to come back to. I don't have a price on my head, so he's afraid I'll give away the location."

"Are there others in town who'd like to leave?"

"Yes."

"Who?"

"I don't think you know any of them. Wives, mostly. Diane Price, for one."

"Max Price's wife? She wants to leave?"

"She wants them both to leave, but he won't. She's tried everything but begging."

"Do you know her well?"

"We've become sort of friends."

"Sort of?"

"She's never been sure whether or not I ever slept with Max. I think it's always in the back of her mind."

"Have you?"

She nodded and said, "Before they were married . . . and once since."

Clint remembered how jealous Max had gotten when he found out that Diane had visited his room—and yet he had slept with Suzanne after marrying Diane.

"It was soon after they got married," she said, reading his mind. "They had a little argument—well, it was more than a little argument. It was the first time she proposed that they leave. They had a fight and he came to the saloon and got drunk, and came upstairs with me. It never happened again after that."

"Because you wouldn't let it, or because he never came around again?"

"He never came around again—and I wouldn't let it if he did. Anyway, he really loves her, Clint."

"I know," he said and explained what had happened after Diane had come to his room.

"Who told him?"

"I don't know for sure, but I can guess."

"Meade!"

"Either he did it or he had it done, probably under orders from Hedge."

"Why?"

"I think they're worried about me, and Max is damned fast with a gun."

"They want you to face each other?"

"Like I said, they must be worried about me."

She put her hand on his thigh and said, "I'm worried about you too. I'd hate to see anything happen to you."

"Because I'm your ticket out?"

She dug her nails into his thigh for a moment, then said, "I'll admit that's part of it, but the other part is more important."

"What's that?"

"This."

She climbed astride him and began rubbing her bristly black bush against his thigh. Slowly, his cock began to swell. When she felt it she began to rub against it, wetting it, coaxing it to grow even bigger. When she felt it pulsing she moved her hips and captured it in one swift movement, slamming down on him so that he entered her to the hilt. She gasped, and then began to ride him wildly. It felt so good for her that she was sobbing by the time her release came, and then he let his boiling joices explode into her with a great groan of his own.

When he awoke the next morning she was on top of him, rubbing her taut brown nipples across his face. He reached out with his tongue to wet them, and then took them into his mouth and sucked them alternately. Her breasts were very firm, like ripe peaches, and he loved sucking on them. Apparently, she enjoyed it as much as he did and had very sensitive nipples, because as he was sucking, her body began to tremble with orgasm.

"Oh, God," she said, still rubbing her tits in his face, "nobody's ever done that to me before."

"Always glad to supply new sensations for the lady," he said, burying his face between her breasts and licking the valley between them.

He turned her over so that she was on the bottom and he was on top and entered her that way. She wrapped her strong, lithe legs around his waist and moved her hips in unison with his until finally they came together in a shattering explosion.

"What will you be doing today?" she asked as he was getting dressed.

"Breakfast first," he said, buckling on his gunbelt, "and then I'll just have to see what develops."

"Do me a favor, huh?"

"What?"

"Don't get yourself killed."

"That's the number one priority on my list of things *not* to do," he assured her.

Chapter Thirty

At the other end of town, Clyde Hogan and Matt Daniels were discussing what their next move should be. Rather, Daniels was arguing, and Clyde Hogan was trying his best to ignore him.

"God damn it!" Daniels yelled. "What's the matter with you, Clyde? Your brother ain't coming. The posse got him."

"Shut up, Matt," Clyde said, menacingly.

"Well face facts, man!" Daniels went on. "We've got a two-way split on our hands, now let's make it and go our separate ways. I don't know what kind of craziness you got planned for this here town, but I don't want any part of it."

Matt Daniels had given up any hope of grabbing all the money for himself. Half looked good enough to him now, and he wanted to get it and get out before Hogan or the Gunsmith or somebody else did something to get him killed.

"Look, if you take half then even if your brother does show up you'll have his share."

"And what should I tell Clayton?"

"Hell, send him after me; I'll take care of him. Clyde, you're acting crazy. The Gunsmith is on our tail, and who knows who else. All I want is my fair share."

"We'll wait one more day," Clyde said. "If Johnny doesn't show by then I'll give you half."

"One more day!" Clyde Hogan said again.

"Fine," Daniels said in exasperation. "I'm going downstairs to have breakfast—unless somebody puts a bullet in my brain before I can eat."

"Enjoy it."

Daniels stormed out of Clyde's room, slamming the door behind him, but Hogan didn't hear the sound it made. He was already lost in his own thoughts.

First and foremost he was worried about his brother. Planning the bank job had been for Johnny's benefit, so that they could settle down before his little brother was forced into the kind of life he himself had been leading since he was sixteen.

On the other hand, he was wondering what Meade and Hedge were waiting for. He knew they wanted his money; why didn't they come and get it?

Unknown to him, the two men were discussing just that subject over at the town hall.

"I think we should go up to his hotel and take the damn money away from him," Meade said. "I can come up with some trumped-up charge."

"I don't want a trumped-up charge," Hedge said. "I want a real charge that will stick."

"Have you got something in mind?"

"Actually, I have," Hedge said with great satisfaction. "Something that will net us Hogan's money, and rid us of Hogan and the Gunsmith, while maintaining our position here in Inferno."

"All that?" Meade asked skeptically.

"All that, Meade."

"What's the plan?"

"Listen carefully . . ."

Clint had breakfast in the hotel dining room, but with the memory of the breakfast he'd had at Max's, he was hard put to enjoy the food they served him.

During breakfast he started to wonder if he was going to be forced into taking a more active role. Should he forget about the other two men and try and take Hogan and his partner? Maybe Russell and the posse had already caught the other two. And what about Demi? How impatient was she getting? How long would it be before she tried something foolish, like finding Inferno herself?

He decided to give it the rest of the day for something to happen. If nothing did, when night fell he'd make his move and try to bring Hogan and his partner out of town in the darkness. He didn't know what would happen when people realized they were gone. Would they assume that they had simply left town during the night on their own? And even if they did think that someone had taken them, would they try to get them back?

And once he got the two men out of town where could he go then? Driftwood certainly wouldn't offer him sanctuary. He was going to have to head for a town with a federal marshal, or an army outpost, to make sure that he'd have the help he needed to stave off a posse from Inferno, and to make sure that something was done about the town immediately.

What was it Demi had said about his plan? That it was crazy? Damned if he wasn't starting to think she might have been right.

Demi Templeton had already displayed more patience than she ever had before in her life, and she had come to the end of it. She had heard nothing from Clint since he left, and how the hell was she supposed to know whether he was in trouble or not?

That's it, she decided. It was time that she did something—anything!

She decided to go to the telegraph office and send a telegram to Phoenix, Texas. Maybe they knew something there. Maybe John Russell had sent them word about where he was, and then she'd be able to contact him and tell him what had happened.

She drafted the message, making it as short and to the point as she could, then gave it to the operator and told him that she would wait for a reply.

"Could be awhile, miss," he said.

"That's all right," she assured him. "I've got nothing else to do."

"Suit yourself," he said, and proceeded to send the message. A half hour later Demi was ready to saddle her horse and go out looking for Clint Adams when the answer came back.

"Here you go, miss," the operator said, handing her the piece of paper on which he had transcribed the answer to her message. "I hope it's what you been waiting for."

The operator, a married man of many years who was not happy about it, examined the woman with open admiration as she read her reply, but then expressed surprise when she muttered, "Shit!" vehemently.

The message was from Sheriff John Russell himself, and it said that he and the posse had returned to Phoenix and called off any further search. That was it, no explanation as to why, which was probably his way of making her pay for going with Clint and not with him.

Demi stood, stunned, as she realized what this meant. There was no help coming for Clint Adams. He was in Inferno alone—if he had even found the town—and there was no one but her to help him get out.

And that's just what she was planning on doing—although for the life of her she didn't know how!

To the dismay of Clint Adams, Clyde Hogan, Matt Daniels, and even the saloon girl, Suzanne, the day went by uneventfully. Clint watched Hogan and his partner, while Clyde and Daniels watched the street for any sign of Johnny Hogan and Dan Clayton. Sheriff Meade watched Hogan and Clint Adams, while Suzanne kept walking to the batwing doors of the saloon to check the street for activity.

Diane Price still had not been confided in by her husband, and Max Price had not mentioned to her that he knew she'd been in Clint Adams's room. There was a strained silence between them that neither knew how to handle. More and more Max Price started to think that maybe it had happened because of the appearance of Clint Adams, and maybe it would go away when he did.

Maybe, he thought on more than one occasion, he should see to it that Clint Adams went away for good.

It was a tense day for a lot of people in Inferno—and for one in Driftwood—and by day's end several of those people had decided to take matters into their own hands.

That was when all hell broke loose!

Chapter Thirty-One

As fate would have it, Clint Adams and Clyde Hogan found themselves in the same saloon at the same time, but it was more than fate that they were once again seated at the same poker table. Once Clint realized that Hogan was there, and playing poker at a table with an empty chair, Clint just sat himself down at the same table and started to play cards.

Matt Daniels was standing at the bar drinking when the Gunsmith entered, and upon Clint's arrival Daniels began to drink more rapidly, with increasing nervousness. Only the thought of his share of the money kept him from mounting his horse and leaving town right then and there. He had agreed with Clyde to give Johnny and Clayton one more day, and now the day was over and they still hadn't arrived. In the morning he and Clyde would divvy up the money and go their separate ways.

Other eyes also noticed that the Gunsmith and Hogan were in the same place at the same time and left to inform Sheriff Meade of that fact.

"All right," Meade told his three special deputies upon receipt of that information. They were "special" because they would do anything for money, including killing a man without a second thought. "You men know what to do."

"Right," one man said, and the other two nodded.

"Well, go and do it then," Meade said, staring at each

man in turn, "and don't mess it up. It ain't everybody who gets a chance to make a name for himself like this."

All three men nodded their agreement. They filed out of the office carrying rifles in addition to their handguns.

Meade left the office too, to go over to Hedge's and tell him that the countdown had started.

"It's your bet," Clint told Clyde Hogan. They were playing seven card stud, and Clint had dealt out five cards. He, Hogan and one of the other three players were still left in the hand. Hogan was sitting with a pair of kings showing and two hearts. The other man had a pair of sevens. Clint was showing a pair of eights.

"Every time we sit down it seems to come down to you and me, don't it?" Hogan asked, watching Clint.

"You've got a lot of patience."

"Hey, I'm still here," the third man said, alternating looks between Clint and Hogan.

Hogan looked at the man and said, "Yeah, and it's gonna cost you to stay longer too. Twenty."

They weren't the biggest stakes that Clint had ever played for, but he knew how expensive it was to stay in Inferno, and it wouldn't pay to throw his money around in a poker game.

The third player looked at the money in the pot in disgust and said, "Damn," throwing his cards in. A pair of sevens could only carry you so far.

"It's up to you, Mr. Adams," Hogan said. If Clint hadn't followed Matt Daniels the night before, he would have been surprised that Hogan knew his name.

"I call."

Clint dealt out the sixth card to each of them, face up. The seventh card would be face down. Hogan's pair of kings remained unchanged, but he bought a third heart. Clint's card was a three of clubs and did nothing to improve his hand.

"You're still boss on board," Clint told Hogan.

Hogan took a peek at his hole cards, something Clint Adams never had to to. He knew that he had a pair of aces under there. He also knew that if Hogan had a third king in the hole, his own aces and eights weren't going to be any good. There was also the possibility that Hogan had the fourth and fifth heart hidden. Clint had watched the cards fall on the table very carefully. He knew that his other two eights had fallen and that one of the aces was gone. His only hope was the case ace, which was a foolish play, but his luck had been good and he decided to go for it.

Hogan spent some time examining his hole cards, which he always did, whether he had something there or not. The younger man was a good player. Patient, and not a tell to his name. A tell was a gambler's giveaway, something a man did or didn't do whenever he had a good hand. Clint had known a man who would stroke his upper lip with the little finger of his left hand any time he thought he had an unbeatable hand. He had even known a man who would cross the first and second fingers of his right hand whenever he was bluffing, as if praying for the luck that would make his bluff work. Hogan had no tells, and that, coupled with his patience, made him a good gambler—at least as far as cards were concerned.

"I'll go for twenty," Hogan finally said, laying his hole cards flat and tossing the money into the pot.

"I'll call," Clint said, eyeing Hogan, "and raise you twenty."

He gave Hogan one bump for the hell of it, and when Hogan raised him back, he knew he was going to need that case ace bad.

"Call," he said, and dealt them each their last card, face down.

Hogan made a big production out of examining his three hole cards, while Clint glanced at his seventh card and then put it down flat alongside the others. He wouldn't have to look at them again.

"Go ahead," he said to Hogan.

Without hesitation Hogan said, "Twenty."

Clint wondered if the money Hogan was playing with had come from the Phoenix bank holdup. In point of fact, it had, which didn't bother Hogan any because he figured on getting back the money he had given Hedge, and more.

Because he was planning on holding up Inferno. . . .

Of course, he had counted on Johnny and Clayton's help, but now it would just be him and Matt Daniels—if he could get Daniels to go along. He didn't figure on that being a problem, though, because he wasn't planning on giving Daniels much of a choice.

It would get done that very night—and he had a new idea about who could help him—but first there was his hand to play out. . . .

"Call your twenty," Clint said, "and raise."

Hogan's face remained expressionless. Clint was sure he had either the three kings or the flush when he called the raise and reraised.

"Fifty more," he said, which brought a murmur from the rest of the room. Clint and Hogan were now the center of attention.

Hogan eyed the money in the pot and nodded to himself, making a decision. "All right," he said. "I'll call. What have you got?"

Clint kept his eyes on Hogan's as he turned over his three hole cards and showed him the three aces. The case ace had been the ace of spades—the death card—but all he was concerned with was that he hadn't ended up with aces and eights, the hand his friend Bill Hickok had been killed while holding.

He hadn't even wanted to *fold* with them.

When Clint decided it was time to quit, he excused himself and stood up, collecting his winnings. He walked to the bar, where Matt Daniels gave him plenty of room, and ordered a beer. He drank it quickly and then left through the batwing doors.

He had gone about twenty feet when he became aware that he was being followed, and he was fairly sure it was Hogan. Maybe the time had finally come for him to make a move.

The street was dark except for the streetlamps. He continued walking toward his hotel, his ears open for the slightest sound from behind him. If Hogan pulled his gun, the Gunsmith would hear the sound of steel against leather. It was a sound he was very familiar with.

Suddenly, there it was, but there was another sound, as well—and then the night was alive with gunfire.

"Look out!" he heard Hogan shout. He turned, hand snaking toward his gun, and he saw Hogan with his gun out, finger squeezing the trigger. As Hogan's gun spat fire, there was the sound of another shot, and Clint looked up on the roof of the general store, where Hogan had been aiming. He saw the man with the rifle catch Hogan's bullet with his chest and fall from the roof to the street below.

Hogan had saved his bacon . . . but it wasn't over yet!

He heard the sound of a round being jacked into the chamber of a rifle and looked across the street. On the roof of another building was a man aiming a rifle at Hogan's back.

"Hogan!" he shouted, squeezing off a shot at the same time. His bullet plowed into the second rifleman, who tumbled backward out of sight. His keen ears picked up another sound. He turned quickly and snapped off a shot at the mouth of an alley. He heard a man grunt, and then saw him stagger into the light and fall to the ground.

The Gunsmith and Hogan stood their ground, guns out and ready, waiting for futher trouble. When none came they looked at each other, guns held at their sides. Clint was determined to let Hogan make the first move, but when he did it wasn't the one he was expecting.

Hogan holstered his gun and ran up to Clint, who holstered his own gun.

"Let's get over to that alley," Hogan said.

They rushed toward the alley as they heard men pouring from the saloon. As they passed the body on the ground, Clint saw his face and remembered it.

"This way," Hogan said, leading the way through the alley and around behind the buildings. He led Clint in a circle until they were behind the Gunsmith's hotel, and then they forced the door and went up the stairs to his room.

When they were in the room Clint started for the lamp. Hogan said, "Keep it low. I don't want too many shadows."

Clint lowered the flame on the lamp so that they had just enough light to see each other.

"You saved my life out there," he said to Hogan. "Why?"

"I followed you out of the saloon because I thought it was time we had a talk. I happened to see the guy on the roof, and he was drawing a bead on your back. I don't like to see any man shot in the back. Besides, you returned the favor pretty quick."

"All right," Clint said, "since you wanted to talk to me, let's talk."

"I don't know why you been watching Matt Daniels and me, but I've got a proposition that might make you forget your reason."

"And what's that?"

Hogan moved closer to Clint so that they could see each other's eyes and said, "I'm going to rob Inferno, and I want you to help me."

Chapter Thirty-Two

"Why do you think I'm here, Hogan?" Clint asked.

"I don't really care why you're here, Adams," Hogan said. "Do you know how much money this town makes? It's supposed to go toward running the town, but a lot of it goes into the pockets of Hedge and Meade."

"Is it in the bank?"

"I don't think so. I think Meade's got a hidden safe in his office."

"That's too bad."

"Why?"

"Because you've got experience with banks, don't you, Hogan?"

Hogan stared at Clint and then asked, "Are you from Phoenix?"

"I was there when you and your boys robbed the bank."

"And you volunteered for the posse?"

"Something like that."

"Look, I convinced Meade and Hedge that I took twenty-five thousand dollars out of the Phoenix bank."

"If I remember correctly, you got ten."

"Right."

"That means you gave Hedge twenty-five hundred?"

"Right again."

"Why?"

"I wanted Hedge and Meade to try and take the rest from me, so I could kill them."

"What have you got against them?"

"It's personal."

"You're asking me to risk my neck to help you rob them? My neck is mighty personal to me too."

"Yeah, but think of the money you'll make."

"What's my share supposed to be?"

Hogan hesitated, then said, "Twenty-five percent."

"Can you get Daniels to go along with that?"

"I can handle Daniels."

Clint thought a moment and then said, "He doesn't know anything about this, does he?"

"No."

"What does he think you're planning to do?"

"Split up the money we took from the bank in the morning."

"Your brother and the other man get here?"

Hogan shook his head and said, "No. Your posse must have gotten them."

"Maybe not. Maybe your brother just can't find the town."

"Yeah," Hogan said, "maybe, but I can't count on that. I've got to do what I came here to do, and then worry about Johnny. What do you say? Will you help me?"

"Just the two of us?"

Hogan shook his head and said, "Daniels will be in when I tell him about the money. It's the only thing in the world he'd risk his neck for. Besides, if you're with us he can stop worrying about you."

"What made you think I'd go along?"

"I didn't, but I knew it would be easier with you along. What about it?"

Clint made a fast decision to go along with Hogan, because he'd have a better chance of getting out of Inferno if Hogan and Daniels were to come willingly. Once they got out, he could turn the tables on them—he hoped.

"Okay, Hogan," Clint said. "I don't know if I'm doing something I'll be sorry for, but I'm in."

"You were a lawman for a long time, weren't you, Adams?"

"Yeah, a long time."

"Ever steal anything?"

"Nothing that wasn't mine."

"Well, this won't be like stealing," Hogan said, "not when you think of who you're stealing it from."

"I'll try and remember that."

Hogan headed for the door. Clint stopped him by saying, "The dead man we passed in the alley—"

"What about him?"

"I recognized him. He was in Meade's office last time I was there."

"One of Meade's deputies?"

Clint nodded. "My guess is they saw a way to get rid of me and you at the same time. Kill one of us and pin it on the other."

"Looks like we put a crimp in that plan, don't it?" Hogan asked.

"Yep," Clint said, "looks like."

"Where have you been?" Daniels demanded when he opened his door in response to a knock and found Hogan standing there. "The saloon emptied out when we heard the shots, and I half expected to find you or Adams on the ground. Instead we found three other guys."

"I killed one of them, Adams killed the other two."

"What happened?"

Hogan started to explain, but before he could finish Daniels broke in and said, "Now I *know* you're crazy. They would have killed the Gunsmith for us."

"And me too. I saved his life, and he saved mine, and now he's throwing in with us."

"Throwing in with us? What are you talking about?"

"Sit down, Matt. I've got something to lay out for you,

and I think you'll see that my way is the best—and most profitable.''

At the word *profitable* Matt Daniels's ears pricked up, and he sat down to listen to what Hogan had to say.

Chapter Thirty-Three

When the knock sounded on Clint's door he knew that it was Hogan coming back with Daniels. He wondered if the other man had come willingly.

"Come on in," he said, opening the door for them.

Hogan walked boldly into the room, apparently confident that he had a partner in the Gunsmith, while Daniels sidled in, watching Clint suspiciously.

"I'm not going to bite you," Clint said to the man.

"You'll have to prove that to me," Daniels replied.

"It's all right, Matt. Don't worry," Hogan said. He looked at Clint and said, "Are you ready?"

"What's your plan?"

"Meade and Hedge will probably be waiting in Hedge's office to hear what happened with Meade's three men."

"Giving each other alibis."

"Right."

"What do they need alibis for?" Daniels asked. "They run the town."

"If the other people in town found out that they were breaking their own rules by stealing *and* killing, they wouldn't be running it anymore," Clint said, and Hogan nodded his agreement.

"We'll go over to the office and throw down on them there. We'll make Hedge open the safe so we can take the money, and then we'll get out of there."

"We gonna kill them?" Daniels asked.

"No!" Clint said before Hogan could answer. Hogan stared at him and Clint said, "If you're planning to kill them in cold blood, I'm out."

"What do you suggest?"

"We can tie them up. We should be long gone by the time they get loose."

"We'd be better off killing them," Daniels said.

"Then I'm out," Clint repeated.

"We'll tie them up," Hogan said. He looked at Daniels and said, "We can't expect him to change his ways all at once, can we?"

"He's killed men before, the way I hear it. You don't get a rep like he's got without doing some killing."

"Not in cold blood," Clint said. "The men I killed deserved it. Besides, I never killed a little girl or a lawman."

"I didn't kill no little girl—" Daniels began angrily, but Hogan cut him off.

"Forget that. We got work to do tonight, so let's get to it."

"It's been too long," Meade complained. "We should have heard something by now."

"Be patient," Hedge said. "They're probably sorting things out. Your men will be here with the shocking news soon enough."

"They better be."

At that point there was a knock on the door and Hedge said to Meade triumphantly, "See? Open the door."

Meade went to the door, opened it and then was sent staggering back by a sharp shove in the chest.

"Hey!"

"Keep your hands where I can see them, Meade!" Clyde Hogan ordered. He turned his gun on Hedge then and said, "You too, Mr. Mayor."

"Hogan!" Hedge said, and then his surprised was doubled when he saw Clint Adams walk in behind the big blond. Matt Daniels was outside keeping watch.

"What's going on?" Hedge demanded, trying to assume control of the situation.

"We'd like to see your safe, Mr. Mayor," Hogan said, "and we don't have time to waste. If you think I won't kill you, just try me. You fellas thought I was a big joke three years ago. Well, now the joke's on you." He pointed his gun at Meade and said, "If he doesn't open the safe in ten seconds I'm gonna kill you first, and then him. I've got nothing to lose."

He stood with his gun trained on Meade, watching the man start to sweat. Clint stood with his back to the door, his thumbs hooked in his gunbelt, letting Hogan play it out his way.

After a few precious seconds had ticked by and Hedge hadn't moved, Meade shouted, "Well, open it, damn it!"

"You'll never get away with this, Hogan. Or you, Adams," Hedge said, in a last ditch effort.

Hogan cocked the hammer on his gun and Meade said, "It's under the desk, in the floor!"

Clint examined the floor and determined the location of the safe. "Excuse me, Mr. Mayor," he said, backing Hedge away from his desk. He put both hands on the edge of the desk and pushed it to the left, away from he panel in the floor that was hiding the safe.

"Open it," he told Hedge.

"You can't—"

"Open it, for God's sake!" Meade shouted.

Hedge frowned, then knelt heavily, opened the wooden panels and twirled the dial on the safe. When he had it open Clint stepped forward and removed the two saddlebags that were hanging over his shoulder.

"Excuse me," he said again, putting his hand on the mayor's chest and pushing him backward. He looked into the safe and found that it was filled with neatly stacked and banded piles of money.

"Looks like you were right, Hogan," Clint said. "These public servants have been stealing from their citizens."

"What do you think would happen to you if we told everyone in town that you've been stealing, and that you tried to have us killed tonight?" Hogan asked, and he continued without waiting for an answer. "They'd rip you apart. You know, I'd like to see that."

"You wouldn't—" Meade stammered.

"Just hold still and be very quiet and maybe I won't," Hogan said. "You got it?"

"Wait," Clint said. He'd been stuffing the saddlebags with the money and had a few more stacks to go. "All right, I've got it all."

"Sit down, Mr. Mayor," Hogan said, gesturing with his gun. "You too, Meade."

"What are you gonna do?" Meade demanded, sitting down.

"Just tie you up for a while, that's all," Hogan said, "althought I'd much rather kill you, myself."

Clint ripped some cord off the curtains in the room and began tying Hedge's hands. He tossed a piece to Hogan, who did the same to Meade.

"Use their belts for their feet," Clint said, and they both secured the feet of their captives to the chairs they were seated in.

"They'll be after us, you know," Hogan said to Clint, holstering his gun.

"By the time they get loose we'll have put plenty of miles between us and them. Besides, they're going to have a lot of explaining to do in order to get anyone to go with them."

"Maybe. It would still be better to kill them."

"No."

They stood facing each other for a few moments, and then Hogan said, "All right, let's get the hell out of here."

They found handkerchiefs on both men and used them as gags; then Clint tossed one full saddlebag to Hogan and moved toward the door. He opened it carefully and peered out, then signaled to Hogan that it was all right for them to leave. Outside Daniels was waiting with their horses, and they mounted up and rode down an alley.

"We can go through this alley and leave town without anyone seeing us," Hogan said.

"How much did we get?" Daniels asked eagerly.

"Don't know," Clint said. "We'll have to count it first chance we get."

"Right," Hogan said, "but first we've got some heavy riding to do, so let's shut up and do it."

Hogan was thinking about Clint Adams and how hard or easy it was going to be to kill him. He had told Daniels to watch him for a signal and he'd let him know when the time was right.

Clint, on the other hand, was thinking about how hard or easy it would be to get the drop on both men, disarm them, tie them and then get them to some town where he'd get help from the law.

Daniels was wondering if he would ever get a chance to kill Hogan after they killed Adams.

So each man was busy with his own thoughts as they sneaked out of town, the first men to ever rob Inferno. The irony of that was not lost on any of them.

Chapter Thirty-Four

They rode for a good piece of the night and when the threat of daybreak started to show they pulled up and lit a fire for coffee and a breakfast of beef jerky and stale biscuits.

"Shouldn't even be making coffee," Hogan said, "but a man needs something to keep himself moving."

"Even if they smell it," Clint said, "they know we're out here anyway. That's no secret."

Daniels was watching Hogan closely, waiting for the signal to kill the Gunsmith, but it was much too early for that. Clint saw Daniels's eyes studying his friend, and it wasn't hard to figure out why.

"Sit and take a load off your feet, Daniels," Clint said, watching him.

Daniels's head jerked at the sound of Clint's voice and he said, "I been setting all night."

"And you'll be sitting all day, or I miss my guess." He looked at Hogan and asked, "What are your travel plans?"

"South."

"There's a town within easy ride of us in any of the other directions," Clint pointed out.

"I know it, but we're heading for Mexico, and we'll split up the money there."

"Hogan, what about your brother?" Clint asked.

Clyde looked at Clint and said, "That's my business. After we split up, I'll find my brother."

"Clyde," Daniels said, "if we head for Mexico we ain't gonna be riding over nothing but flat for days."

"I know."

"Well, we didn't stock up on supplies before we left."

"I got enough for a little while. Before we run out we ought to come to a small town called Comanche Wells. We should be able to pick up some supplies there."

Daniels frowned and said, "You been that way before?"

"I been that way before."

The way he said it made it obvious that he didn't want to talk about the past.

"You want some coffee, Matt?"

"We should keep riding," Daniels said nervously.

"If you're nervous, go on up on top of that rise and keep an eye out behind us."

"Yeah, that may be a good idea."

Daniels left and Hogan handed Clint a cup of coffee. "If they start after us I don't think they'd do it before morning," he said. "It would take Meade and Hedge that long to talk their way out of the jam we left them in."

"You think they will?"

"Hedge is a mighty good talker," Hogan said. "That's why we should have killed him."

"If you wanted to kill him, you would have."

"You're right."

"You want him to hunt you for a while before you kill him."

"Right again."

"Well, I guess the whys and wherefores of that are your business—"

"That's right."

"Well," Clint said again, "when it comes to a point where I've got to risk my neck, those whys and wherefores are going to become my business and I'll expect to hear about them."

"When the time's right."

"If I'm not dead before then."

Hogan frowned and said, "What do you mean by that?"

"Daniels is watching you for the word to throw down on me; only he wouldn't be doing that if he thought he was going to be alone. He expects you to back him."

"I ain't concerned with what he expects."

"We made a bargain and I expect you to stick by it."

"That's kind of the way I feel about you too, Adams. Guess we got at least that in common."

"I guess so."

Clint looked up at the rise where Daniels was standing and caught Daniels looking at him. When Daniels saw him he turned and looked away at the trail behind them.

Hogan was right. After Hedge and Meade had finally worked themselves loose they'd had to cook up a story between them that the rest of the town would believe. They convinced ten men that Clint Adams and Clyde Hogan had killed the three men on the street—which was no lie—and then broken into the mayor's office and robbed them—again, which was no lie. They just didn't tell any of them *what* was stolen. It was enough that two men who had been given the hospitality of Inferno had decided to return it with treachery.

One of the men Hedge and Meade convinced to come with them was Max Price, because Price was still stewing about his wife having gone to see Clint in his room. He wanted to resolve that situation so he could stop thinking about it, and this seemed the best way. It never dawned on him just to ask Diane about it.

They started out the next morning, twelve men led ostensibly by Meade, although Hedge was the one giving the orders. It was Hedge who said, "They'll head south, because we got ears in the towns all around us. They'll head south, toward Mexico."

"We'll get them," Meade said.

"Yeah," Hedge said, while the two men were standing alone, "but we can't afford to take them alive, not Adams, not Hogan and not his friend, Daniels. Make sure, Meade, that the men know that they're to shoot first and talk later. I don't want any of those three men to be taken alive.''

"I'll tell them,'' Meade said. 'They're as good as dead.''

Chapter Thirty-Five

A couple of days later three weary, hungry men rode into Comanche Wells, three men who were growing very tired of each other's company.

Matt Daniels was confused. He and Hogan had had many opportunities to gun down the Gunsmith, and not once had the signal come from Hogan. On top of that, Daniels had not been able to get Hogan alone to ask him why. He figured his first chance for that would come when they got to Comanche Wells.

Clint felt like he was going cross-eyed from trying to watch both men at one time, and he figured that maybe Comanche Wells was the place to take their guns from them.

Hogan's mind was occupied half the time by thoughts of his brother Johnny. The other half of the time he was wondering how far he'd be able to trust Daniels once Adams was dead, and the answer was not very far.

The town was small and had only a token sheriff, a man who supposedly would uphold the law as long as he could do it from a sitting position. This information was supplied by Hogan, further proof that he had been this way before, and had planned on coming this way all along. Clint recognized the fact that he and Daniels had been used by Clyde Hogan for his own benefit, and he wondered when Daniels would realize the same thing.

147

"We'd better get some supplies and keep moving," Hogan said.

"What about fresh horses?" Daniels asked.

"We'll get them," Hogan said, "but we'll pay for them, Daniels. We'll do this my way."

"Sure, Clyde, sure."

"Suppose you get the supplies, Matt, and Adams and I will get the horses."

This further puzzled Daniels. Why was Clyde pairing off with Adams and sending him for the supplies? Was Clyde planning a double-cross? How could Clyde expect to take the Gunsmith if he killed Daniels first? Hogan had something up his sleeve, but Daniels wasn't sure he could wait to find out what it was.

Clint and Hogan went over to the livery and looked at the horses that were available there.

"Not much to pick from," Hogan said.

"All we get's horses from men like you, passing through and in need of fresh mounts," the liveryman said. "I care for them and just wait for the next drifter."

"At least they're fresh," Clint said. "How about that bay?" he asked Hogan. "And that one there, and the sorrel."

"All right," Hogan said to the liveryman. "You heard him. Make me a price and then we'll switch our gear."

Clint left Hogan to haggle with the liveryman and watched from a few feet off. He too was wondering what was on Hogan's mind. Had he forgotten about his brother and what happened in Phoenix? Was Russell still out there with the posse? he wondered. And what was Demi Templeton up to?

When the deal was made Hogan and Clint walked their horses over to the corral and made the switch. They rode back over to the general store to pick up Daniels and his purchases.

On the way Clint said, "You've sure got Daniels confused."

"How's that?"

"He's still waiting for the signal from you to kill me."

"Maybe that's why I haven't given it," Hogan said.

"Why, because he's waiting?"

"No," Hogan said, "because you are."

They met Daniels and divvied up the purchases, so that each man was carrying some of the supplies. They couldn't afford to be slowed down by a packhorse.

"Maybe we better clear something up," Hogan said to the two of them before they started out.

"Like what?" Daniels asked, wondering why Hogan was going to speak out in front of Adams.

"The three of us need each other," Hogan said, "so let's all stop waiting for a chance to kill the other."

"What are you talking about?" Daniels asked, incredulous.

"You know what I'm talking about, Matt. There's got to be a posse on our trail from Inferno, if we can call it a posse. If they catch up to us we're going to need every gun we've got. There's enough money for all of us to share, so let's start trusting each other for a change." He waited for the other two men to think about what he said and then asked, "What about it?"

"Sure, Hogan," Clint said.

Daniels looked at both Clint and Hogan and then said, "Whatever you say, Clyde."

"All right. Why don't we go over to the saloon for a quick drink on it before we move out?"

Both Clint and Daniels agreed, and they rode to the town's lone saloon.

Chapter Thirty-Six

The three men stood at the bar with their drinks—beer for Clint and Hogan, whiskey for Daniels, who drank it almost with desperation. In spite of Hogan's speech and their apparent acceptance of what he had said, it was obvious that they were ill at ease with each other.

As Daniels ordered a second whiskey from the Mexican bartender a back door opened and a girl stepped out. She was young and pretty, with full breasts barely contained by a low-cut peasant blouse, and long black hair. She saw the three men and watched them with interest. She smiled and postured for them. The bartender said, "That ees my daughter. She ees pretty, no?"

"She is pretty, yes," Matt Daniels said. He looked at the old man behind the bar and asked, "How much?"

"Five dollars?" the man asked hopefully.

Daniels looked at the girl again, trying to determine if she was worth the investment. She took a deep breath, causing her breasts to strain the material of her blouse even farther. He decided that she would be. Clint studied her and came to the conclusion that she was a remarkably developed sixteen.

"We don't have time for that," Hogan said.

"You're the one who said that they wouldn't start after us until morning," Daniels reminded him, "and that gives us at least a six-hour head start. That plus the fact that they won't know what direction we've taken." He indicated the well-endowed girl and said, "You mean to tell me that you don't have time for a pretty girl like that?"

Hogan looked at the girl and felt something stir inside of him.

"All right," he said, finally. "Go ahead." Hogan looked at Clint and said, "What about you?"

"No thanks," Clint said. "She's a little closer to your age than she is to mine. I'll just take a table and wait."

Hogan remained at the bar while Clint took a table, and Daniels went with the girl into the back room. After fifteen minutes he came out, hitching up his pants and grinning, and Hogan went into the room. Daniels got himself a drink and joined Clint at the table.

"You don't know what you're missing, Adams," he said, still grinning. "That little Mex gal was really something. She like to turned me inside out."

"I'm glad you enjoyed yourself."

Daniels looked at Clint and suddenly realized that he was sitting there talking to the Gunsmith like he was any other man and not a man that he was waiting to kill.

"Don't worry, Daniels," Clint said, "I'm still not going to bite you."

"I ain't worried," Daniels said, trying to appear confident. "I mean, we're partners, ain't we?"

"Sure, Daniels," Clint said, "we're partners."

Hogan's need must have been even greater than Daniels's because he took twice as long. When he came out he wasn't grinning, but Clint sensed that he was not as tense.

The girl came out behind him, holding her money in her little hand, and eyed Clint confidently. When it was obvious that he wasn't going to get up and indulge, she pouted and took the money to her father.

"Her own father selling her," Clint said, in disgust. "I think we'd better get a move on, gents. We can't waste any more time."

"This wasn't no waste," Daniels said cockily, standing up. "You're the one who wasted time. You could have gone in there with her too."

"I'll try to console myself," Clint said, standing up.

They left the saloon, mounted up and rode out of town, heading south toward Mexico, three men all wondering what their next move should be.

Demi Templeton was riding almost aimlessly. The only thing she did know was the direction Clint was headed when he left Driftwood, and she kept going that way, hoping against hope that she'd be able to help him somehow and that help was on the way behind her.

The "posse" led by Hedge and Meade came upon a spot where Clint, Hogan and Daniels had stopped to camp.

"They're headed for Mexico, all right," Max Price said. "Good guess, Meade."

"It was no guess, Price," Meade said, exchanging glances with Hedge.

"I still can't understand why they did it," Price said.

"We don't have to understand," Meade said, "we just have to catch up to them . . . and kill them!"

Max Price was about to object but found that the rest of the men agreed with Meade. Adams, Hogan and Daniels had broken the rules of Inferno, and they had to pay.

"We've got to catch them first," was all he said.

"If they're on their way to Mexico from here," Hedge said, "they'll have to pass through Comanche Wells."

"Why?" Price asked.

"It's the only place where they can get supplies, and they left town in too much of a hurry to have stocked up." Hedge leaned on his saddlehorn and said, "If they're in Comanche Wells now, we can beat them to the border."

"We can?" Meade said.

"There's a shorter route," Hedge said. "We can be there before them . . . waiting for them."

Chapter Thirty-Seven

"The border is over that rise," Hogan said, pulling his horse to a stop.

"What are we stopping for?" Daniels asked.

"I want to split the money here and go our separate ways," Hogan answered.

"What? I thought you wanted to do that in Mexico." Daniels said.

"I changed my mind," Hogan said, swinging down from his horse.

"Hogan, you're acting crazier and crazier," Daniels said, moving forward. For a split second he was between Clint and Hogan, and the Gunsmith did not see Hogan come out of his saddlebag with a gun.

"Hold it right there, Adams," Hogan snapped, pointing the gun at him.

"Well, it's about time!" Daniels said.

"Keep quiet and get his guns, Matt."

Daniels rode up alongside of Clint and relieved him of his forty-five and rifle. He missed the twenty-two New Line Colt inside Clint's shirt, tucked into his waistband. He backed away, holding the Gunsmith's guns.

"All right," he told Hogan, "go ahead and kill him."

Hogan looked like he was just about to do that—and Clint was steeling himself to go for his hideout gun—when they heard a shot and a bullet kicked up dust from the ground between them.

"What the hell?" Daniels snapped. They all looked up and saw a dozen riders come over the rise from the direction of the border, and they recognized Meade and Hedge leading them.

"God damn it, how'd they get here before us?" Daniels asked.

"No time for that," Hogan said. "Let's ride!"

They had forgotten about wanting to kill Clint Adams. All three men wheeled their horses around and started to run from the posse. Clint stuck with Hogan and Daniels because they had his guns, and because they were all in the same predicament. Three men with guns were better equipped to hold off a dozen than two were—now all he had to do was get them to give him back his guns.

As they rode they could hear the shots from behind, and the occasional hiss of a bullet passing very close by them. Clint was sorry he didn't have Duke beneath him, because the big boy could have outrun any of the horses coming from behind.

"Over there!" Clint yelled, pointing. There was a stand of brush and rocks that would offer cover, and they headed for it.

They dismounted and walked their horses behind the boulders with them.

"We'll have to try and stand them off," Clint said. Their horses were too tired to outrun the posse. This was the only way.

"Hogan, you better give me my guns," Clint said as the men got closer.

"No!" Daniels shouted.

"They're coming fast, Daniels. You and Hogan think you can hold them off by yourselves, be my guest and give it one hell of a try."

Hogan and Daniels glanced at each other, but when a hail of lead began to fall around them, he nodded and Daniels tossed Clint his guns.

"Let's get started," Clint shouted. He holstered his gun, levered a round into the Springfield's chamber and began to fire.

The twelve mounted men wasted no time in finding cover of their own. They dismounted and scattered.

"Hold your fire!" Clint yelled. Daniels kept firing, though, and he had to shout again before the man stopped.

"Now what?" Daniels demanded.

"Now it's up to them," Clint said. "They can rush us or wait us out. I think they'll wait."

"And what do we do?"

"We wait too, my friend," the Gunsmith said, "unless you want to try rushing them."

"Christ," Daniels said in disgust, and asked again "How'd they get to the border ahead of us?"

"Hedge must know a short route," Hogan said.

"And you didn't figure on that, right?" Clint asked. "Sonny, you're got a lot to learn—I only hope you're got some time left to learn it."

Clint decided not to talk anymore and just to watch and listen . . . and wait.

Chapter Thirty-Eight

Hedge and Meade had found cover close to each other. Meade called out, "Now what do we do?"

"We can sit and wait them out, or we can rush them," Hedge said. "If we rush them we're gonna lose some men, and if we wait we'll be here forever, because they must have picked up some supplies in Comanche Wells."

"Sounds like a helluva choice," Meade said.

"Well, we've got to make it our come up with something else," Hedge told him."

"Why don't we just lay down some fire in there and see if we can't hit something."

"You're the sheriff," Hedge said, "give the order."

Meade did, and for a few minutes the twelve men sent a hail of lead toward the three men behind the rocks, hoping to come up with a ricochet hit. When they stopped to reload Meade called a halt, and Hedge decided to try and make contact.

"Jesus!" Daniels shouted as the shower of lead came their way.

"Stay down low," Clint called out to them. "They could get lucky with a ricochet."

As luck would have it, a bullet sent a sliver of stone into Clint's left bicep. It stung, and when he pulled it out the wound bled some, but it wasn't serious.

As suddenly as the barrage of lead had started it stopped, and Clint heard a man's voice call out. "Hogan!"

"That's Hedge," Hogan said.

"Hogan, this is Mayor Hedge!"

"He sounds very formal," Clint said.

"He's got to put on a show for the rest of them," Hogan replied.

"You haven't got a chance, Hogan," Hedge shouted. "Come out with your hands up and you'll get a fair trial."

"Is he serious?" Clint asked. "A fair trial in Inferno?"

"He's serious," Hogan said, "and he would be the fair and imparital judge."

"Terrific," Daniels said. "we got a lot to look forward to."

"The only thing I'm looking forward to is getting out of here with my skin intact," Clint said pointedly, which had a double meaning that he hoped would not escape the other two men.

It didn't.

"Hogan! Answer me."

"Let him stew," Daniels said.

"No, talk to him," Clint said. "See how he wants to play it. The fact that he's playing himself up as mayor means that all those men aren't his. We may be able to use that to get out of here."

"Whether they're his or not," Daniels said, "none of them are angels, you know."

"Talk to him," Clint said again, and Hogan nodded.

"I hear you, Hedge!"

"Come on out, Hogan. We can work something out."

"Sure," Hogan replied, "like you'll let us dig our own graves before you kill us. No thanks!"

"Don't be foolish. You stole some money, sure, but your main offense was breaking the rules of Inferno. You'll have to pay a fine for that, but—"

"Yeah, like our lives," Hogan said, cutting Hedge off. "Don't make me laugh, Hedge."

"*Some money*," Daniels said, hefting the saddlebag he was carrying that held half of it.

"Have we counted that money yet?" Clint asked.

"There's at least fifty thousand dollars in here," Daniels said, indicating his saddlebags.

"About the same in mine," Hogan said. His saddlebags were still on his horse.

"A hundred thousand dollars," Clint said, not without a certain amount of reverence. "That's *some* money, all right."

"They've got to kill us just to keep us from talking," Hogan said.

"I agree," Clint said. "They're not going to let us walk out of here."

"I think we should make a run for it," Daniels said.

"Their animals have to be in better shape than ours," Clint said. "You want to take a chance, be my guest. I won't stop you."

"Just leave the money here," Hogan added.

"Ha, no way—"

"Then keep quiet and let us think," Clint said.

Daniels subsided and Clint assessed the situation. All around them the land was flat. There wasn't even any way one of them could sneak around behind the twelve men and try to scare off their horses. They were pinned down in the middle of nowhere with apparently no hope of getting out, and no hope of getting any help.

An hour later Daniels was starting to fidget restlessly, complaining of leg cramps.

"Stay off your feet and they won't cramp," Clint said. He had noticed that Daniels was unable to relax. For the most part he remained in a squat position, as if he were constantly prepared to run. Clint and Hogan either remained on their knees or sat on the ground.

"I can't take this anymore," Daniels complained bitterly.

"Make a run for it," Hogan invited.

"Sure, you'd like that, wouldn't you?" Daniels demanded. "Then you could split with Adams instead of me."

"You think it makes a difference?" Clint asked. "I'm sure he'd rather split with neither of us."

"Sure, take it all," Daniels said. "Was that your plan, Hogan? First we kill Adams and then you kill me?"

"If you didn't kill me first," Hogan said. "Don't think I didn't know what you had on your mind all along."

"Why don't you two fellas just shoot each other now and save our friends the trouble," Clint suggested.

"Well, you're the one who wanted to be left alone to think," Daniels said accusingly, "and you haven't come up with one idea yet."

"He's right," Hogan said. "We can only wait so long."

"And *they* can only wait so long. Whatever supplies they have must be split twelve ways, and we only have to split ours three ways."

"Yeah, but they probably have more," Hogan said.

"Sure, they have more than we have of everything, including short tempers."

"You think they're fighting among themselves now, the way we are?" Hogan asked.

"I hope so. I've never seen a bunch of men yet who couldn't find something to fight over when thrown together for long periods of time."

"So you're saying we should just keep waiting?"

"That's what I'm saying."

As darkness started to fall Meade called out to Hedge, "It's getting dark."

"I don't need you to tell me that," the mayor replied.

"Well, what are we going to do?"

"For one thing you're going to continue to look like you're in charge here. You are the sheriff, you know."

"I ain't a real sheriff, damn it!" Meade snapped, remembering what Clint Adams had said to him about that. "Sometimes I feel like a damned lawman, and I hate lawmen."

"Settle down."

"Some of the men are getting restless. Some of them want to turn back."

"We can't let them. This has to look like it was done right," Hedge said, lowering his voice even more. "If anyone finds out about that money we're finished."

"What are we gonna do, then? How can we flush them out?"

"We'll have to send some of the men to circle around behind them. We ain't gonna be able to wait them out like I thought. Adams is too experienced to make some kind of a wrong move. Pick out some men and tell them to get behind them. If we can do that we might be able to force them out."

"Right."

"Hey," Daniels said suddenly, "something's going on."

Clint looked up and saw that some of Hedge and Meade's men were moving slowly toward their horses.

"Start firing," he said curtly. "If they get to those horses they can get around behind us."

The three men began working their rifles as quickly as they could, firing at the crawling men. The men scrambled back to their hiding places as bullets kicked the dust around their feet.

"Well, that ought to bring one point across to them," Clint said, reloading.

"What's that?" Daniels asked.

"They're just as pinned down as we are."

"We're just as pinned down as they are," Meade told Hedge. "What now?"

"Shut up and let me think," Hedge said irritably.

There had to be some way to get those three men out in the open where they could be cut down. If not, he and Meade might end up being killed by their own posse!

Chapter Thirty-Nine

Each side built a fire, and while it was possible to periodically shoot at the other fire in the hopes of hitting someone who was around it, generally they decided that it would be a waste of good lead. Lead was the one thing they couldn't afford to waste, because it was the one thing they couldn't do without. If their food ran out or their water, they'd get hungry or thirsty, but if their lead gave out . . . they'd be dead.

As daybreak came the men who were standing watch woke the others. Shots were fired from both sides just to keep all concerned on their toes.

"Somebody's got to come up with an idea," Daniels insisted at one point. "I mean, somebody has got to come up with an offer."

"At which point the other side would come up with a counter offer," Clint said. "Good idea, Daniels."

"It is?"

"What have you got in mind?" Hogan asked.

"David and Goliath."

"What?"

"One man against one man for everything," he said. "The money and our lives."

"You think Hedge or Meade will go for that?"

"Maybe not, but maybe the other men will insist on it."

"And who would you suggest represent us?" Hogan asked, eyeing the Gunsmith suspiciously.

Clint smiled at them and said, "Well, I'll leave that to you boys."

"You think you're the logical choice, don't you?" Hogan asked.

"Well, I might tend to make the other man nervous, don't you think?"

"I don't like it," Daniels said.

"For once I agree with you," Hogan said. "What's to stop you from making a deal for yourself once you step out there?"

"What's to stop them from gunning me down once I step out in the open?" Clint demanded. "It works both ways."

"There's got to be another way," Daniels said.

Clint thought a moment and then said, "There is."

"What?"

"Listen . . . ."

"HEDGE!"

Meade looked at Hedge when the voice sounded; it was the first time either side had spoken since the night before.

"That's Hogan," Hedge said.

"What's he want?"

"Let's find out."

"Hedge!"

"I hear you, Hogan."

"I've got a proposition."

"Let's hear it."

"One man from your side and one from ours, winner take all!"

"Is he crazy?" Meade asked. "He knows we won't go for that."

"Yeah, but he also figures the others will."

Meade turned around and looked at the other men, some of whom were looking at each other and nodding.

"It's better than sitting here for another day and a half," Max Price called out, and he was probably speaking for the others.

"What do we do?" Meade hissed at Hedge.

"I guess we'll go for it."

"But you know who they'll use."

Hedge nodded and said, "The Gunsmith, of course. And we'll use Price."

"Price!" Meade said, his eyes lighting up. Then he frowned and asked, "But can he take him?"

"We'll find out, won't we?"

"All right, so they went for it," Hogan said.

"They had to."

"So now you'll step out there in the open . . . ."

". . . and you'll do your part," Clint finished for Clyde Hogan. "If you don't, I might get killed. If I do, that will solve one problem for you, but it might also get you killed as well."

"This is crazy," Daniels said, but Hogan gave him a look, and he went on— "but we'll do our part."

"Why me?"

"Because Max Price is the only man here—maybe the only man I know of—who would stand a chance against the Gunsmith," Hedge said.

He had called for Price to come forward, and since Price had heard the entire arrangement being made, he knew what was coming.

"Did you ever ask him what your wife was doing in his hotel room?" Meade asked.

"Meade—" Hedge said warningly, and the sheriff fell silent. He had told Price about the incident, not wanting to leave it to one of his men. Maybe it would work for them now.

"Price, you've built something in Inferno, and you've done it without your gun," Hedge said.

"I know."

"Well, we've all built something there, but now we might need your gun to help us keep it. Is that too much to ask?"

Price didn't answer. He now wondered why he had never asked Diane about that incident. Maybe if he had, he wouldn't be faced with this decision now.

"It's up to you, Max," Hedge said. "We can go back home, or we can give it all up."

"Going back home means killing the Gunsmith."

"And the other two."

"But, you made a deal—"

"If they get away with it, others will try. Maybe some of these. We've got to keep that from happening."

"If a man came sniffing around my wife . . ." Meade said under his breath but loud enough for Hedge and Price to hear.

"All right," Price said. "All right."

Chapter Forty

"Hedge!" Hogan shouted. "We're ready!"

"So are we!"

"Send out your man!"

"You send out yours."

"Okay," Clint said to Hogan. "I'll step out first. Just be ready."

"We're ready," Hogan said, holding the reins of his horse.

Clint stood up and stepped out into the open, tensed against the possible impact of dozens of chunks of hot lead. When none were immediately forthcoming, he relaxed and waited for their man to step out.

Max Price! Clint thought about what he had told Diane Price, and muttered, "Damn Max."

Price began to walk toward him. Clint brought his mind back to the task at hand, hoping that he wouldn't have to break his word to Diane Price.

Clint started walking and stopped when he thought he was still too far from Hedge and the others to be heard. Price kept walking, and when he stopped he was close enough to Clint to hear him when he spoke normally.

"Hello, Max."

"I'm sorry it has to be this way, Clint. Believe me I am."

"I won't draw on you, Max."

"Then why are you out here, Clint?" Max said. "I'm going to have to kill you."

"I won't draw on you, but I did come out here for a reason. Actually, I'm glad it's you they sent out here. I can reason with you."

"What are you talking about?"

"I've got something to show you that will convince you that Meade and Hedge have been stealing Inferno blind for a long time."

"What?"

"It's true. They've been using their positions to get rich off of you and the others."

"You have proof?"

"That's why we're out here."

Clint lifted his right hand up, knowing he was taking a chance. Price could have chosen that moment to go for his gun, but he didn't, and Clint gave Hogan the signal.

"What the hell are they waiting for?" Hedge asked irritably.

"Are they talking to each other?" Meade asked, squinting to get a better look.

They both saw Clint Adams raise his hand, and then suddenly a horse was running toward the pair from where Hogan and Daniels were hidden.

"What the hell?" Hedge said.

They watched as the horse ran toward the two men, who abandoned their intentions of killing each other, to catch the horse. When they caught it, Clint Adams appeared to be showing Price something in the saddlebags.

"Hedge—"

"Meade—"

"What are they doing?"

"I'm not sure, but have your gun ready. . . ."

"How much is there?" Price asked.

"Fifty thousand in this bag," Clint said, "and at least that much in the other."

"Over a hundred thousand dollars?"

"That's right."

"How do I know that you didn't just steal back your own money?"

"You mean that maybe me—or Hogan—gave this to Hedge as ten percent of one of our jobs? Wouldn't everyone in Inferno have heard about a job that big? Or even two jobs that added up to that?"

"Or three," Price said, peering at the money in the bag.

Price looked convinced, and Clint thought that maybe it was going to work.

"Let's get on with it," Price said.

"What?"

"I said let's get on with it. Send the horse back to your friends."

"Max, what are you saying?"

"Clint, you just gave me my out," Price said. "You just showed me how to get out of the kitchen."

"I thought you liked the life you were leading."

"Diane wanted me to give up my guns, Clint. You know what that would mean to men like us, right? Instant death. So we compromised. We opened the café and I wore my guns, but I wore an apron too. It was all right for a while, but it started to wear thin pretty fast. Now you've shown me the way out."

"How?"

"That money."

"I don't understand."

"All I've got to do is kill you, help Hedge and Meade get rid of those other two, and then we'll be the only three who know about the money."

"And for a share, you'll keep quiet."

"For half, and they can just go on running Inferno the way they see fit, because Diane and me will be gone."

"Max, this doesn't sound like you."

"Clint, you never really knew me. We haven't seen each other in so many years that you know me less than you did back then." Price pointed to the money and said, "For that much money, I'd do almost anything, and if getting it means killing you, then let's get on with it."

Everything had gone wrong so fast that Clint couldn't believe it. Price backed up a bit, slapping the horse on the rump so that it trotted out of the way, and then backed away again farther.

"Let's get it over with."

"Max, think this over."

"I can't afford to think it over, Clint," Price said, "because I might change my mind. A thing like this has to be done right off. Now let's do it."

When the two men backed off from each other it was obvious that they were going to go ahead.

Hedge and Meade took their hands off their guns and watched with great anticipation.

Hogan and Daniels watched in confusion.

"It didn't work," Daniels said. "What the hell do we do now?"

"He's on his own," Hogan said. "All we can do is watch."

They all watched as the two men faced each other. The outcome was in no doubt for only one man, and he had made a promise to a woman that he was now going to have to break . . . or die.

They all watched the blur that was Max Price's hand as it moved toward his gun, and they thought that they had never seen anything that fast . . . until the Gunsmith drew!

As fast as Price's hand seemed to be just a split second earlier, now it appeared to have frozen in midair. The Gunsmith's gun spat death, and the slug struck Price in the chest before his hand could touch his gun.

Clint didn't waste any time. As soon as he fired he took off at a dead run back toward the rock where Hogan and Daniels were waiting. He heard the shots behind him as the stunned men suddenly began firing. The slugs slammed into the dirt just behind his heels, and as he approached the rocks he took off in a flat-out dive.

"What went wrong?" Hogan demanded as Clint righted himself.

"We got the wrong man."

"He decided to go for the money himself, didn't he?" Hogan asked.

"Yeah, he did," Clint said, adding to himself, *And he made me break a promise.*

"Any man faced with that much money is the wrong man, Adams," Hogan said. "So much for your big idea."

"Hedge made a deal; let's see if he intends to stick to it."

But they all knew he wouldn't. They were in the same position they had been before, except that they were facing eleven men instead of twelve.

Demi Templeton was close enough to hear the shots. She stopped her horse so she could listen and pinpoint the location, and then dug her heels into the animal's haunches to urge him on in that direction.

She knew instinctively that it was Clint Adams and he needed help, and she hoped she wouldn't be too late.

Nearby three men also heard the shots. After exchanging glances they agreed on the location and started off at a gallop. Their hope was the same as Demi Templeton's—that they would not be too late to help.

Chapter Forty-One

Frustrated because Price had failed to outdraw the Gunsmith, Hedge and Meade immediately opened fire on Clint Adams, and the rest of the posse simply followed their lead. After Clint had made it back to cover safely, Meade gave the order to keep firing, and while seven of them fired, four others ran for their horses and made it.

"That's great," Daniels said, watching the four riders. "They'll come around behind us now, and we're as good as dead."

"We might as well go out blazing," Hogan said.

"Talking about blazing," Clint said, "what about the money?"

"What about it?" Daniels demanded.

"Well, if they kill us," Clint said, firing an occasional shot by popping up and down during the barrage, "they'll get the money."

"So what are you proposing?" Hogan said, shouting to be heard over the gunshots.

"Burn it!"

"What?" Daniels said, incredulous—so incredulous that he forgot to duck and a bullet came dangerously close to hitting him. He dropped down out of sight and said, "You're crazy. That's a hundred thousand dollars!"

"Do you want Meade and Hedge to get it?"

Daniels didn't answer, but Hogan said, "No, I don't."

"Well," Clint said, ducking down as the barrage continued, "burn it."

Hogan thought a moment, then nodded. "Cover me."

They couldn't lay down much cover, not with two guns against seven, and it was largely by luck and speed that Hogan made it back to safety with the two saddlebags.

"Dump it out," Clint said.

Hogan dumped out first one bag, and then the other, and the packets of neatly banded money lay in a large pile, waiting . . . .

"You can't," Daniels said.

"Even if we're dead, they won't win," Hogan said.

"Let's make a run for it, Clyde. *Anything*, but don't burn it!"

Suddenly there were shots coming from behind them, and they could see the other four men lying flat on the ground and firing.

"Make a decision, Hogan," he said.

He stared at the Gunsmith for a few seconds and then said, "Got a match?"

Caught in the crossfire the three men split their efforts, firing first in one direction and then the other. A ricochet caught Daniels in the left side, and a bullet creased Hogan's right shoulder.

"Looks like this is it," Clint said aloud, but he was talking to himself more than to the others. He'd found Inferno and given it his best shot, and it had come to this. Maybe he would be better off standing up and going out with gun blazing. That was a hell of a lot better than the way Hickok and some others had bought it.

Suddenly, there was a change in the sound of the shooting. As loud as it had been, it was now louder, as if more guns had joined the battle.

"Something's happening," Clint shouted. He popped his head up, looked around, and finally saw what was happening.

"Look!" Daniels said, spotting it at the same time.

From one direction there was a lone rider heading toward

the four men at their back, firing as it rode. As it got closer Daniels shouted, "It's a woman."

"Demi," Clint whispered.

"And look there!" Hogan said.

From another direction three riders were closing in on the seven men in front of them, and those men now turned to meet their charge.

"Start firing!" Clint yelled. "We may get out of this yet."

While Hogan and Daniels fired toward Hedge, Meade and their men, Clint ran to his horse and mounted. He urged the animal on toward the four men who had circled around them, because Demi seemed to be trying to take them all on alone.

The men had seen her and were turning to fire. Clint drew his gun on a dead run and began firing. One shot caught a man in the back, spinning him around and dumping him on the ground. Demi fired as the men turned toward Clint, confused about which way to look, and her shot took off the top of another man's head.

The two remaining men couldn't decide which of them to fire at. They began to look around for their horses in the hopes of getting away. They each fell prey to a bullet, one from Clint's gun and one from Demi's. Clint and Demi met amid the four dead men.

"Clint? Are you all right?"

"I'm fine, thanks to you." He turned in his saddle to look behind them, where a fire battle was still taking place.

"Who are those three men?"

"Friends of yours."

"Of mine?"

"When you didn't get in touch I sent another telegram to your friend Frank Leslie. He sent one to a man named Hartman in Labyrinth, Texas* and he sent one to Dodge City—"*

"The Mastersons!" Clint said.

*The Gunsmith #14: Dead Man's Hand
*The Gunsmith #20: The Dodge City Gang

Chapter Forty-Two

The appearance of the Mastersons—Bat and Ed—and Bill Tilghman, all friends of Clint Adams's and all lawmen from Dodge City, had been so sudden that Hedge, Meade and their men had not had time to recover. They had tried to fight back but found themselves the victims of a crossfire, as Hogan and Daniels continued to pump lead.

Both Hedge and Meade were dead, as were five others. From the original posse of twelve, only two remained, and they were wounded.

"I'm glad you boys just happened along the way you did," Clint said, after friendly embraces had been shared all around.

"Happened along, hell," Bat Masterson said. Still in his twenties Bat Masterson had forged himself a reputation many would have stood alongside that of the Gunsmith—although Bat had not yet become a legend. His brother Ed was a year younger, and Bill Tilghman was of an age with them. "We got a message that your fat was in the fire, so we came to pull it out."

"And you did that, all right," Clint said.

"Who's the young lady?" Ed Masterson asked, as all three young men cast admiring glances at Demi.

173

"I'm the one who made sure you got the message about his fat," she said.

"Demi, you explain it to them. I want to talk to somebody."

While she explained how they had come to get the message, Clint walked about, checking bodies. It was then that he found Hedge and Meade. He looked at the men and said, "Looks like Inferno is going to need a new sheriff and a new mayor. Sorry you won't be there to see the election—or the burning of the town."

When they got back to a town with a telegraph Clint would send a message with Inferno's location. A large force would be sent to burn it to the ground, and round up as many of its "citizens" as they could. But first he would get word back to Suzanne and Diane Price, so that they could get out in time.

The Gunsmith walked over to where he had been hiding with Hogan and Daniels. He found Daniels bleeding from a belly wound, as well as the one in his left side.

"Caught one, eh?" he asked, squatting down next to the mortally wounded man.

"Caught one, hell," Daniels gasped. "It was Hogan who plugged me."

"Hogan?"

"That's right. Soon as he saw that help had come he shot me and started throwing dirt on that burning money. He left the ashes," Daniels said, and Clint looked over at the pile. "He said that was our share."

"Then in the confusion he rode off. Where, Daniels? Where was he headed?"

"Like he said, he headed for Mexico. Get him, Adams. Get that bastard."

Daniels's eyes glazed over, and then, eyes wide, he died.

Clint rose and walked back to where his friends were waiting.

"Hogan got away," he told Demi. "He's got the bank money and some of theirs." He indicated the men on the ground.

"Have you been in Inferno all this time?" she asked.

"Inferno?" Bat Masterson said.

"You found Inferno?"

"Yes, I found it, and if you're real nice to these two men they'll give you the location, I'm sure."

"Give us the location?" Bat said. "And where are you going?"

"I'm going after Clyde Hogan, the man who started me off on this whole thing. When you get to a town with a telegraph send a message with the location of Inferno. The faster we can get the army out there, the better."

"Will do," Bat said. "Which way did this jasper go?"

"Mexico."

"Want some company?" Tilghman asked.

"You fellas have done enough. I can take care of this part by myself."

"Not without me," Demi said. "I've been sitting around too long waiting for you."

"The two of us, then. You fellas can handle it here, can't you?"

"Get going, pard," Bat said, "and we'll see you in Dodge, right?"

"You won't believe this, Bat," Clint said, shaking his head, "but that's where I was headed when this whole thing started."

Clint took a horse from one of the dead men, and he and Demi started riding south. He told her what had happened in Inferno—leaving out references to Suzanne—and then she told him what she had done before leaving Driftwood to look for him.

"It was smart of you to telegraph Frank," he said. "He knows who my friends are in Texas."

"You're not going to like what the telegram from Phoenix said," she warned.

"Go ahead and tell me. It can't be any worse than what I've already been through."

"My reply came from John Russell."

"Russell! He's back in Phoenix?"

"He's back, and with the man who killed Jenny."

"But I thought Hogan—"

"It was Hogan's younger brother Johnny who rode Jenny down, Clint," she explained. "John and the rest of the posse came across Johnny Hogan and another man named Clayton riding around aimlessly, looking for Inferno."

"So the kid did get lost."

"Lost and panicking. So panicked that when the posse caught up to him he admitted everything. John was satisfied to have Jenny's killer and decided to let the money go."

"I'm sure the town fathers will love him for that."

"They were outraged about the way Jenny was killed," she said. "They'll probably accept his decision to return without the money."

"Well, there's still the question of who killed Ramsey, and since I know who has the money, we might as well recover it."

"How much did he get on top of the bank money?"

Clint explained how they had robbed Hedge's office, how much money they'd gotten, and how they'd agreed to burn it when they all thought they were going to die.

"Burn that much money?"

"They didn't want Hedge to get it, and it was sort of a minor victory for me, as well."

"So he saved however much he could, shot his friend and took off for Mexico."

"I don't think Matt Daniels and Clyde Hogan were friends in any sense of the word, Demi. I think once they had disposed of me, it was only a matter of time before one killed the other."

"So now the only one left is Clyde."

"And somehow I just can't find it in me to let him get away," Clint said, "not after everything I've been through."

"Everything we've been through," she corrected him. "You don't think it was easy sitting around that jerkwater town waiting to find out what happened to you, do you?"

"You mean there were no men there?"

"It would serve you right if I had taken a man, just to pass the time, but I didn't," she said. "Which just goes to show you how—"

"—loyal you are?"

She stared at him a moment, then smiled broadly and said, "I guess that's as good a word for it as any."

Chapter Forty-Three

They tracked Clyde Hogan for five long days. After all that time even Clint and Demi were getting on one another's nerves. But their patience paid off when they began to find more sign.

"He's getting sloppy," Demi said, looking at the ground. "Cigarette butts, fires left to burn out on their own."

She looked up at Clint and said, "He thinks he's thrown us. He thinks he's in the clear."

"Either that, or he just doesn't care anymore. Come on, mount up and let's keep moving. I have a hunch he's going to be waiting for us somewhere."

"Waiting to ambush us, you mean?" she asked, climbing astride her horse.

"No, I mean . . . just waiting. By now he must know that his brother is dead or as good as dead."

They had gotten the word by telegram two days earlier of Johnny Hogan's hanging.

"He waited so long for that kid to show up. . . . Come on, we're wasting time."

The next town they came to was called Santa Domingo. When they asked the liveryman if a stranger had ridden into town he said, "*Sí, señor*. Two days ago."

"When did he leave?" Clint asked.

"He has not left, *señor*."

"He's still here?" Demi asked.

"*Sí, señorita*. His horse is still here."

"Where is he?"

"They say the giant with the yellow hair has not left the cantina since his arrival, *señor*. Perhaps you will find him there."

"Perhaps. *Gracias*."

"*Por nada, señor*."

They left him their horses and started walking to the cantina.

"What are we gonna do if he's there?" Demi asked.

"Take him back to Phoenix, hopefully with the money."

"Clint?"

"Yes?"

"What will we do with the extra money?"

"I was thinking . . ."

"Yes?"

"It won't make up for her loss, but I was thinking of giving it to your sister."

"I was hoping you'd say that."

"On the condition that she doesn't marry John Russell . . . ever. I don't want him getting his hands on that money. I've got a score to settle with him."

"For what?"

"For leaving members of his posse to die."

Demi sensed how angry Clint was about that point and decided not to discuss it with him further.

When they reached the cantina Clint said, "You wait out here—"

"Oh, no, I'm not going through that again," she said, cutting him off. "Where you go, I go, *amigo*."

"All right, come on."

When they walked into the cantina they immediately saw Hogan sitting at a corner table with his face buried in his arms. He could have very well been asleep.

The place was a shambles, and it was empty. Apparently Hogan was the kind of drunk who busted up furniture. Virtually the only pieces still intact were the table and chair he was occupying. The bartender, a meek, thin Mexican with watery eyes, looked hopefully at Clint while shining a glass so hard Clint thought it was going to shatter in his hands. Clint jerked his head at the bartender, who didn't need any further coaxing. He dropped the glass to the floor and ran out the door.

When the glass shattered Hogan lifted his head with a jerk and looked bleary-eyed around the room.

" 'Nother drink,'' he yelled.

"Go behind the bar,'' Clint told Demi in a low tone, and she obeyed.

"I want 'nother drink!'' Hogan bellowed, slamming his massive fists down on the table. The wooden legs groaned in protest but withstood the pounding.

He looked at the bar. When he saw Demi he grinned stupidly and said, "A lady bartender. Will you get me a drink, lady bartender?''

"No more drir.ks for you, Clyde,'' Clint said, approaching the table.

"Whazat? Whozat?'' Hogan said, squinting at Clint as if trying to bring his face into focus. "Izzat you, Adams?''

"It's me.''

"Well, get a bottle and pull up a chair, old buddy. We're celebrating.''

"What are we celebrating?'' Clint asked, but Clyde Hogan didn't hear him.

"If we can ever get a drink we can celebrate,'' he muttered.

"Clyde, you have to come back to Phoenix with us,'' Clint said, speaking very slowly and loudly, as he would to a child.

"Why? So they can hang me the way they hung Johnny?'' Hogan demanded.

"You know about that?''

"I heard there was a hanging. Who else would they hang?'' When Clint didn't reply Hogan asked, "They did hang him, didn't they?''

"They did.''

"Well, I been waiting for you to get here. What took you so long?''

"Where's the money, Clyde?"

"The money."

"Yes, the money you took from the bank and the money we took from Hedge. Where is it?"

"In a safe place."

"Where?"

Hogan frowned, as if trying to remember, and then he brightened and said, "Behind the bar," pointing with his right hand.

Demi looked underneath the bar and saw two saddlebags there. Looking inside of them she found the money, some of which was black and sooty. "It's here."

"Okay, Clyde, come with us."

"You got the money, Adams, what you need me for?"

"To stand trial."

"And get hung?" He shook his big, flat head and said, "Ain't nobody gonna hang Hammerhead Hogan. You never called me that, did you, Adams? Hammerhead Hogan."

"No, I never did."

"You know, you and me could have been friends if we met at a different time."

"Maybe, Clyde, but right now I've got to bring you back with me."

"No. You gotta kill me."

"No, I don't, Clyde. There's no need—"

"Yes!" Hogan shouted. "Yes, there is a need! They hung Johnny!"

"That doesn't mean you have to die too—"

"Johnny shouldn't have died," Hogan said. "I'm the one who should have died, got hung."

"Why, Clyde? Why should they have hung you?"

"Johnny didn't do it."

"He didn't do what, Clyde?"

"He didn't kill that little girl."

"He confessed," Demi said.

"Ah! He told the others—Daniels and Clayton—he told them he did it too, but he didn't ride down that little girl."

"Who did?" Demi asked.

Hogan slammed his fist into his chest and said, "Me, I did

it. That's why you gotta kill me, Adams. Johnny got hung for something I did. Don't you see?''

"Clyde—"

Hogan stood up then, picked up the chair and threw it against a wall, shattering it. "You gotta kill me!"

"No, Clyde—" Clint started to say, but he got no further. Hogan, bigger and stronger than Clint, picked him up and threw him the way he'd throw the chair. Clint hit the wall and fell to the floor, and through the haze he saw Demi draw her gun.

"No!" he called.

"Kill me," Clyde Hogan said, staring down at him. "Draw your gun and kill me."

"Clyde, wait—" Clint said, trying to get up. Hogan grabbed him by both shoulders, propelling him toward a group of broken chairs and tables. Clint fell hard, the leg of a chair digging into his side. He cried out.

"Kill me!" Hogan shouted.

"Clint?" Demi called.

Clint, unable to speak, shook his head and hoped that Demi would understand.

"Clyde, you've got to listen to me—" he croaked.

"No, no more talk," Hogan said. "Kill me, Adams, or I'll kill you, and then I'll kill your lady friend."

"Damn it, Clyde—"

With a roar of rage and pain Clyde Hogan charged the Gunsmith again and picked him up like a rag doll. Clint felt powerless in the hands of the big man; he would not allow himself to be beaten to death but did not want to shoot him. As Hogan started to squeeze him in a bear hug, Clint drew back his head and butted Hogan on the nose. The younger man bellowed and grabbed for his bleeding nose, dropping Clint to the floor. From a prone position the Gunsmith hooked Hogan's ankle with his feet and twisted, causing the young giant to drop to the floor. Clint's hand closed over the broken leg of a chair, and then slammed it over Hogan's head. Hogan grunted, stared at Clint for a moment before his eyes blurred, and blacked out.

Demi ran to Clint's side and asked, "Are you all right?"

"Yes, I'm fine," he said. "Just a little winded."

"I'd give you a chair to sit in," she said, "but there ain't any."

"Just give me a minute," he said, bending over and putting his hands on his knees. "Why don't you go and see if this town has a lawman?"

"If it did, don't you think he would have been here by now?"

"We don't need him, just see if he's got any wristlocks we can put on Hogan before he wakes up."

"Oh, all right. Are you sure you'll be okay?"

"Positive. I'm going to get a drink."

Clint straightened up and started for the bar. Watching him, Demi said, "You're all right," and left to find a lawman.

Clint walked around behind the bar, grabbed a bottle of whiskey and took a swig out of it.

No wonder Clyde wanted to die. His younger brother, whom he had obviously loved, had died in his place at the end of a rope. Clyde didn't want to live anymore, but he didn't want to buy it that way, so he'd hoped to force the Gunsmith into killing him. That was why he had waited in this cantina for two days, consuming what must have been incredible amounts of whiskey. Given time, the big man probably would have drunk himself to death.

Clint wondered how hard it was going to be to get Hogan back to Phoenix. If the man wanted to die he'd be making attempts all the way there to get himself killed. Clint had transported men who wanted to escape but never anyone who wanted to be killed. He wondered if he would be able to avoid it.

He was taking another swig from the whiskey bottle, upending it and looking up at the ceiling, when he heard Demi's voice call, "Clint!"

Instinctively the Gunsmith dropped the bottle and his hand streaked for his gun, but Hogan's gun—which both Clint and Demi had stupidly left in his holster, a testimony to their fatigue—was already out and pointed at the Gunsmith. The man was angry because the Gunsmith had refused to kill him, and in his anger—and pain, both mental and physical—he wanted to get even with him.

Hogan cocked the hammer of the gun, a sound which Clint heard while he was drawing his. Then there was the sound of one single shot, and Clint tensed, waiting for the impact of the bullet. When it didn't come he was forced to conclude that he had not been shot dead. He looked at Hogan, and saw the blond giant lying on the floor with blood leaking from a hole in his head. At the entrance of the cantina stood Demi with her gun out, staring at the dead man.

"Nice shot," Clint said.

"He was going to kill you."

"Well, he didn't, thanks to you."

"He's a big man," she went on, "I figured the only way to be sure was with a head shot."

"Good choice." Clint grabbed another bottle of whiskey and rounded the bar to approach her.

"Here," he said, holding it out. "Put the gun away and have a drink."

She holstered her gun slowly, then took the bottle and upended it, taking a healthy swallow. She choked, but kept it down and handed the bottle back.

"I couldn't find a lawman, or anyone who had chains," she finally said.

"That's okay," he answered, preparing to take another drink himself. "We won't need them."

GREAT BOOKS

E-BOOKS

AUDIOBOOKS

& MORE

Visit us today

www.speakingvolumes.us